GHOST STORIES
FROM
THE RAJ

D1535517

GHOST STORIES

FROM
THE RAJ

Edited by
RUSKIN BOND

Rupa & Co

First published 2002
Fourth Impression 2005

Published by
Rupa & Co
7/16, Ansari Road, Daryaganj,
New Delhi 110 002

Sales Centres:

Allahabad Bangalore Chandigarh Chennai
Hyderabad Jaipur Kathmandu
Kolkata Mumbai Pune

Typeset in 12 pts. Simoncini Garamond by
Nikita Overseas Pvt Ltd,
1410 Chiranjiv Tower,
43 Nehru Place,
New Delhi 110 019

Printed in India by
Rekha Printers Pvt Ltd.
A-102/1 Okhla Industrial Area, Phase-II
New Delhi-110 020

Dedication

To Jai Shankar
in memory of those ghostly
twilight walks across
Dehra's old parade ground.

Contents

Introduction

THE *RAISON D'ÊTRE* FOR TELLING A GHOST STORY WAS probably best summed up by the Fat Boy in *Pickwick Papers*, when he said: "I wants to make your flesh creep!"

But it isn't always as simple as that, and not all ghosts are frightening.

The other night I woke up around midnight with bright moonlight streaming in at the window and lighting up the bedroom. Someone, or something—a vague, nebulous figure—was standing beside my bed, looking down at me. It could only have been a ghost. I waited for the spectre to say something but it remained silent; nor did it move away.

"Hello," I said. "And what can I do for you?"

No answer. Not even a gesture, either of goodwill or ill-will. A most ineffective ghost.

"Do you have a message for me?" I asked. "Anything you'd like me to do for you?"

No response. It just stood there, shimmering in the moonlight.

"Well," I said, "I've got better things to do than just lie here holding a one-sided conversation." And I turned over and went to sleep again.

* * *

The ghosts in this collection are far more alarming. Most of them were observed, experienced or imagined by British writers during the period 1840 to 1940: a century of ghosts! The British are a phlegmatic people, not given to displaying much emotion or excitement, with the result that their supernatural experiences are quite convincing when put down on paper. When C.A. Kincaid of the Indian Civil Service described people who turned into panthers (or vice-versa), and mischievous spirits who entered the bodies of straitlaced Englishmen, we have to believe him. As we believe those who found themselves in haunted dak bungalows, graveyards, villages, forests, forts…. Haunted India, in fact! For the British, coming from a land where haunted houses and castles were the norm, were fascinated by the wonderful variety of supernatural manifestations that they found in India: *churails* (the ghosts of wayward women, whose feet always faced backwards), *munjias* (the spirits of Brahmin youths who died before marriage), *bhoots* who took up residence in peepal trees, or mischievous *prets* (Indian poltergeists) who sometimes entered the homes of living people and created havoc in their lives. When I was a boy, one such *pret* took up residence in my grandfather's house and made life hell for everyone—throwing dishes around, knocking pictures off walls, pulling the cat by the tail, and tying knots in my Uncle Ken's pyjamas—so much so, that we had to move to another house for a time. But the *pret* followed us and would not leave until it had been propitiated with the help of a wandering mendicant. He taught me the following useful mantra:

Bhut, pret, pisach, dana,
Shiv ka kehna, sab nikal jana!
(Ghosts and spirits in house or tree,
In Shiv's great name we bid thee flee!)

Amongst the writers represented here, two were keen observers of Indian customs and folklore: Lt. Col. Sleeman, an administrator who, in the mid-nineteenth century helped eliminate the menace of the Thugs, a sect who waylaid and murdered innocent travellers; and C.A. Kincaid, one of the more enlightened of British officials, who wrote sympathetic books and essays on Shivaji, the Rani of Jhansi, and other heroic figures. Kipling, poet of Empire, wrote the occasional ghost story; as did Alice Perrin, wife of an Indian official; her stories were quite popular in the 1920s. In *Caulfield's Crime*, she reveals the more arrogant, cruel aspect of the colonial official. In *The Summoning of Arnold* she demonstrates that the spirits of the dead recognise no frontiers. Ghosts require no passports. They are truly universal beings! Kincaid brings a touch of humour to his stories, but this does not lessen their dramatic impact. The stories of this period tell us something about colonial attitudes—ranging from the paternalistic to the cynically indifferent—but we must remember that they were written purely to entertain, to enliven a dull railway journey, a sleepless night, a rainy day in the hills, a long sea voyage, or a period of recuperation from a tiring illness. Ghost stories are meant to frighten you, but at the back of your mind you know it's all a nightmare from which you are going to wake. In other words, it's a "safe" fear and you can enjoy the process of being frightened.

Doctor Johnson once said of the supernatural: "All argument is against it, but all belief is for it." Those of us who enjoy reading ghost stories are the people who half believe or want to believe. Those who are already convinced of the existence of ghosts usually look for 'factual' accounts rather than fiction. Unfortunately these factual accounts are usually very dull and consist of "sightings" of unusual phenomena, rather like the sightings of UFOs, unidentified flying objects, whose reconnoitrings are singularly without interest or purpose.

The human imagination is a wonderful thing, and I shall conclude this brief introduction with a 'factual' experience of my own, which was certainly hair-raising.

Some years ago, a neighbour of mine, an old English lady who lived alone, died of heart failure and was laid out on her bed for the night, as it was too late for the funeral. A friend and I decided that we would take turns at her beside, and at about midnight I sat down on an easy chair in the bedroom to undertake my part of the vigil. There had been the usual power failure, but we had lit candles and I could see the features of the corpse quite clearly.

For some reason I couldn't take my eyes off her face. Her eyes were closed, but after a while I was sure I could make out a slight smile on her lips. This smile gradually grew wider until it became a rather menacing grin. I was frightened out of my wits. Was I about to see her rising from the dead? As the grin grew even wider, I got up from my chair, ready to flee the room. Just then there was a loud report, like a pop-gun going off, and her false teeth shot out of her mouth and rolled off the bed.

We had forgotten to remove her false teeth. *Rigor mortis* having set in, the rigidity of her jaws had forced her mouth into that terrifying grin, ejecting the teeth with considerable force.

Not a ghost story, but a ghostly one all the same.

Happy hauntings!

Ruskin Bond
1 August 2002

The Wondrous Narrative of John Cambell
Gunfounder to the Mogul Emperors, 1654–1667

A MONGST THE MSS. TREASURES IN THE BRITISH MUSEUM ARE a number of contemporary manuscripts relating to Englishmen who dwelt or travelled in India during the Seventeenth Century. Ranking high amongst them in interest, if not in veracity is one called the Richard Bell MSS. from its having been inscribed by a traveller of that name in the years 1669–1670.

The document purports to contain an exact account of the travels and adventures of one John Cambell who met Bell at Alleppo in 1669 whilst on his way home overland from India and continued the journey in company as far as Rome, meeting with more wondrous adventures on the way. During this journey the narrative was written to the dictation of Cambell and completed at Rome on the 20th December 1670 the joint signatures being attested by Joseph Kent, the English Consul.

How this manuscript came into the collection of Sir Hans Sloane, from which it passed into the British Museum in the year 1780, there is nothing to show, nor why it should have remained unknown to all but the curators until it was discovered by that indefatigable antiquary Sir Richard Temple in the year 1905 and published in the Indian Antiquary of that year, which we have permission to use. Concerning Cambell, Sir Richard Temple thus writes:

"Some of Cambell's statements explain why travellers' tales have become a byword and synonym for pure invention. There is no chronological sequence and anachronisms are frequent. Indeed were it not for the testimony of Manucci who mentions several of the persons alluded to by Cambell it would be difficult to attach any credence at all to the narrative. However, the records of the English in India of this date are so scanty that any account by an eyewitness is worthy of reproduction, and especially so, when, as in this case, out-of-the-way information is blended with accounts of magical occurrences wondrously described." To this William Irvine, the Translator of Manucci, adds:

"This is a wild and utterly unchronological narrative, by the side of which the wildest flights of Manucci read as sober sense. But there are some grains of fact, as the men whom he mentions Robert Smith, John White, Thomas Roach and William Gates are all mentioned by Manucci as with Shah Jehan and Aurungzebe when Cambell was with Murad Baksh and Dara Shekoh, Smith and Roach also appear in the Surat Records in 1667 and 1672 and the son of the latter is mentioned in 1704."

In these, both men are mentioned as having considerable influence at court notably Smith "who has the ear of the Mogul". They were also men of considerable wealth, apparently for these first two letters concern large sums they had advanced to the Company's merchants at Agra on private accounts and of which they were applying to the Company to recover for them. They do not figure very creditably in the pages of the Venetian adventurer Manucci, who was himself a gunner in the service of Dara Shekoh, a son of Shah Jehan, for he alleges that they tried to rob him of the effects of Lord Bard after the death of the latter to whom Manucci had been page. Though Manucci is circumstantial enough it seems that he exaggerates for these men were then high in the service of Shah Jehan and acted by his orders.

However, there seems little doubt but that, like all such men in the service of Indian princes at this period, *might* meant right. From the opening decade of the Seventeenth Century Europeans were entertained in considerable numbers at the Mogul courts both by the reigning Emperors and their sons, each of whom had his personal army, the artillery of which was worked or supervised by European master gunners, mostly runaway seamen from the vessels of the various East Indian Companies, Dutch, English, and French, or ex-pirates wrecked or marooned on the coasts.

So early as 1612 William Hawkins headed some 60 of all nations in a procession to the Catholic Church at Agra the occasion being the baptism of two nephews of Jehanghir willing to embrace a new faith in the hope of those Portuguese brides which had been promised them. However as the brides were not forthcoming, the bargain was cancelled. These Europeans comprised all sorts of trades and professions, such as jewellers, lapidaries, surgeons, doctors, painters and sculptors, though the great bulk were always artillerymen and military artificers, of whom at the period of which we write there were over 200 in the various services.

All received high pay for the time ranging from Rs. 200 to 300 a month, the captain gunners, such as Roach and Smith, drawing much more. The salary of John Whelo, master gunner, in 1712 is recorded as equal to about Rs. 2,000 a month by the Dutch ambassador, so probably Smith and Roach may have been paid almost as liberally if not quite. As a special inducement for European gunners to enter and remain in such service the Mahomedan rulers as to spirituous liquor were relaxed in their case, they being permitted not only to distil, but to sell such liquor to non-Mussalmans, the privilege was valuable for Manucci records that he himself drew Rs. 300 a month for the use of his. Of the origin of the privilege he tells the following amusing story:

"Finding that his own gunners were of no use and hearing that Europeans were very expert at the art, Jehanghir ordered his Governor at the Port of Surat to procure him a master gunner, from the English who were the very first to arrive at this port. They sent him a most skilful gunner who was assigned Rs. 500 a month. But this man, like all the other Englishmen, was very fond of spirituous liquor, and, this being forbidden by the Mahomedan religion, he was consequently very unhappy. Therefore he set about to obtain his heart's desire so, one day when Jehanghir ordered him to fire a shot at a great sheet stretched on sticks on the opposite bank of the river, he intentionally missed every shot."

"At this the Emperor was much put out thinking the man unskilful, and sending for him asked him the reason for such bad shooting when he had such a reputation for skill. The Englishman replied that there was no lack of skill, but that he was unable to see straight unless he had drunk spirits. On this the Emperor directed some to be brought from the elephant stables where there was no lack of it on account of it being kept to give to the elephants to increase their courage in battle or fighting with each other. When the Englishman saw the spirits he was highly delighted, and seizing the bottle put it to his mouth with the same eagerness as a thirty stag would rush to a crystal spring."

"Then at one draught he swallowed the lot licking his moustache for the few drops that clung to it. The Emperor was astounded at the pleasure of the Englishman who expressed his satisfaction by all kinds of gestures. He then went to his gun and after rubbing his eyes told the Emperor they were now clear, and directed that the sheet should be taken away and an earthen pot on a stick put in its place. At the very first shot he knocked the pot to pieces. Therefore in consequence of this amazing skill derived from spirituous liquor, the Emperor gave the Europeans the sole privilege of distilling liquor with which none were to interfere. He said that the Englishmen must have been created at the same time as spirits as without them they were as fish out of water."

The only appearance of Cambell in the records of the East India Company is a mention of his arrival at Bundar Abbas in

January 1669 in poor condition having been robbed of Rs. 8,000 and a quantity of jewels whilst on his way through Sind to Tatta whence he took boat for Bunder Abbas. The letter goes on to say that Cambell had served the Mogul for a number of years and concludes by stating that he had been advanced money and since departed for Alleppo with a recommendation to the English Consul there. It is difficult to decide Cambell's real nationality. In his own account and the mention by the Factor, with whom Cambell claimed relationship the name is thus spelt, and he also writes concerning rich relations in England. But against this is set a statement that though he put the English coat of arms on all the guns he cast for the Emperors, on the trunnions he cast a lion rampant, which was the Scotch crest.

Whatever else he may have been, however, John Cambell ranks very high amongst tellers of travellers' tales of the Baron Muchausen or Sir John Maundeville school. Though he emulates the worthy Sir John in the matter of two headed men and men with eyes in their necks or foreheads, Cambell far excels him in the matter of monstrous beings of unmortal origin who slay whole armies in a single afternoon, of chance met wizards who transmute the money in his pouch to base metal or completely empty it from a distance with other as wondrous feats. But most of all does Cambell revel in tales on Jinns and Demons who pay visits in state or drop in casually on an afternoon or evening for theological and family discussions, and reward their entertainers, or unwilling hosts with revelations of the hiding places of vast treasures.

But with all Cambell's extravagance much that is useful may be extracted from his wonderful tales, for undoubtedly he did serve the Moguls and equally did he make extensive travels in India, Persia and Asia Minor. We have spent much time in reducing his chaotic tale to some chronological sequence and a measure of actual fact, the clue seeming to be in that the narrative was written over a period of eighteen months or so, at many different places, and haphazard, just as the facts were recalled to the mind of the dictator, or his imagination most lively. Judging by internal evidence both narrator and scribe seem to have indulged rather freely in the beverage so relished by Jehanghir's gunner. It must also be remembered that in those days when works of fiction were unknown actual travellers were relied on for tales of the wonderful. Nobly some of them met the demand.

However, the overture is finished, the lights grow dim and on the silver screen of the narrative appears a burly bearded figure whose blackly burnt visage is relieved by blue eyes twinkling with broad humour and perchance a tongue bulging a cheek of brass. A moment's pause. Cambell composes his face to prim decorum and then, over the fancy bridged gulf of some 250 years sounds this wondrous narrative of marvellous experiences.

"You should know that, in the year 1609. Jehanghir being then the Great Mogul, one Asaf Khan being then his Counsel in chief (Commander in chief) had gotten great treasures by his war with the Gentues (Hindoos). It was always their pride to adorn their Pagodays and places where they keep their Gods with images of golden cows and such other creatures as they worship and to embellish these places with precious things of great value. This Asaf Khan plundered them all and by such means got great store of Treasure which he buried in his house at Old Dilly.

After he died, the Emperor by torturing all his generation got six elephant loads of treasure valuing £500.000 though suspicion caused that to this day much remayneth behind, though where, unknown. The only one of his generation now remayning called the Lord Jaffir Khan, a Colonel of Horse (mansabdar) being in great distress of money, comes to the undermentioned, Mr. Robert Smith, Mr. Thomas Roach, Mr. John White, Mr. William Gates and I John Cambell, telling us that if we would lend him a certain sum he would pawn to us his house in Old Dilly a good pennyworth (valuable).

We having lent him this sum, along comes an old Brahmin once servant to him who buried the riches telling us 'within this house is great treasure which ye, being Xtians may dig, for the Emperor not calling you to account as he would us, should we dig and find he will kill us and all our families. But ye may dig and fear nothing.'

So hearing, we agreed with the Lord Khan to dig giving him one share and each taking one. This house was in Old Dilly, we living in Johnabad (Jehanghirabad, the city of Jehanghir). It is as big as Whitehall and Scotch yard (Scotland Yard) together being built Castle wise and very strong. Then for three months we dug and found nothing for they had built house upon house until in the end we came to near nine fathom deep. In this time two of our labourers were struck dead, some broke arms and legs, others lamed and many hurried out (ran away). Presently the Emperor Aurungzebe hearing of our digging sent word to know what we were about.

To which Thomas Roach replied we were digging for stone to build a house withal, this making colour (a blind) and so that passed. Finding more men we continued one more month digging until finding naught, I John Cambell demanded back my money again. Then said the Lord Jaffir Khan.

'Fear naught. I will bring magicians, and if then we find not, you may again have back your money.'

Then he brought three magicians to whom we shewed how far we had digged. After this they did something we understood not casting spells or what not, and then told us.

'Take up this stone,'

This we did and under it found a great brass pot full of money. Said the magicians.

'Meddle not with this now. Leave it until the next day when we will come again to guard you from the Divells, under whose care it be.'

But we obeyed them not, for which we paid dearly. That night we were very merry judging we had found the prize we sought, until in the middlemost of our mirth there came into the courtyard, which was very great, a vast number of labourers with mattocks, spades, and other digging implements, all of *silver* with which they threw up a great mound for a platform. This done, others came and spread carpets after which came nine seeming men bearing a canopie of state having staves of silver which they set upon the top of the mound. We being struck dumb at such sight, remained silent for the space of one hour.

It being the 12 of then night in came a Great Divell in the shape of man, he sitting in a Golden Chair borne on men's shoulders.

He had over him an umbrella with a Gold Staff and Red silken covering, and with him came many other seeming men attending upon him. At this we were all sadly amazed I John Cambell falling into a swoon but soon recovering. Then all we five Xtians having with us Bibles, fell to reading very seriously keeping in our midst the Lord Khan for fear of the Divell. Seeing this, to us said this Divell:

'Lay by your bibles and give me this man who is my *gholam* (slave).'

We kept silent. Then came a great ill-shaped monster into our midst and tried to hawl away the Lord Khan. On this Mr. Smith, our Minister (Elder of their church) stept out and laying his bible on the Monster, made him give up his hold. Mr. White questioned the Great Divell why came he into our house. On this he answered:

'I am Murteza Ally, now the Governor of this part of the Divells world. What do you Xtians here?'

To which Mr. Roach answered: 'We are here of our right. We gave money for this house.'

Then said the Great Divell: 'Let be get you gone from here and with you your bibles leaving my *gholam*, and you shall have all your money back again and three times more.'

To this answered Mr. Roach: 'We know there is much money here. We shall have all or nothing.'

And so consented Mr. Smith, Mr. White, Mr. Gates and I John Cambell. At these bold answers the great Divell raged furiously and told us:

'Ye may thank Isa Musa (Christ) that I cannot withhold this treasure from you ye being Xtians. But ye shall pay dearly for it in the end!'

(Which said threatening came to pass, for a slave girl belonging to Mr. Roach, discovered to the Emperor that we had been digging for treasure and only by great payments did we come free of trouble.) At last said the Great Divell:

'Take your bible away from the Lord Khan and give him to me. He is my slave.'

But we would not whereon up came another ill shap't Monster who demanded the Lord Khan, saying he had been servant to the Lord Khan who buried the treasure and by him slain to prevent discovery. When we would not yield him he raged, saying furiously:

'Then ye shall have nothing.'

On this Mr. White calling him Divell, demanded his departure whereat he again raged, saying:

'I am no Divell but a poor slave that was killed to guard this treasure. Have a care what you say. Why come you here to cast guns and make war. Get you gone to your own country.'

Then said Mr. Roach: 'We will not go save with this treasure.'

So saying we all commenced to read our bibles aloud. On which they all vanished away leaving us swooning from which we recovered not until the coming of the day. When we had awakened we found at our heads something of that for which we had digged being a Golden Image in the shape of a cow with three strings of jewels hanging from it. This discovery we kept secret, melting the gold down to ingots. The next day, I John Cambell going from my house in Johnabad to Old Dilly, was met by a Divell seeming man, riding on a horse which said to me:

'Go no more to Old Dilly to dig or 'twill be the worse for you,' and vanish't away.

'The same night came the Divells to the house of Mr. Roach wherein was the Lord Khan, and cast both over the walls though no harm done, save to the Lord Khan who was bruised full sore. But they molested none of us after so long as we kept our bibles with us, nor even the Lord Khan after we laid a bible on his chest. So, being warned in such fashion we went to the house no more by night but digged only by day, and the dwelling in a tent without the walls. On one afternoon when so engaged there came the Great Divell without attendance and remained by Mr. Smith reasoning (debating?) for three hours by the clock in which time he came and went three several times. He in this discourse told us that his kind have no manlike feelings nor pain, and said they delight much in guarding treasures and dwelling in great gardens, living in ancient and holy trees. To Mr. Smith he said:

'Why do you give your bible to my people (Mussalmans)? Ye are Xtians. Keep ye to your own religion. Meddle not with that of others.' To which Mr. Smith made reply:

'Our religion is free to all that desire it. Begone thou in the name of the Father, the Son, and the Holy Ghost.'

At this the Great Divell said: 'I am Emperor of Emperors, and have great armies and riches at my command. But I have no power over Xtians. Get you gone to your own country.'

But Mr. Smith, again reading from his bible, said 'Avaunt thee Satan!' At which the Divell gave a great howl and vanish't away, coming no more that day. But in the evening when we were all being merry in the house of Mr. Smith, there came suddenly in a Great Sarpent, the colour of Gold which took three turns on its belly and then vanish't quite away. After that there came in a great number of Divells all in terrible shapes some being seeming Tygers some Lyons and divers, other Monsters, most terrible to behold. But we steadfastly reading in our bibles all this time they made us no harm but presently all vanish't away and came no more leaving us in peace to dig the treasure.

'What we got was great but much more remains. When we had got all we desired we cleared (filled in?) the ruins making a fair Garden for the Great Divell according to promise made by Mr. Smith, which said garden at this day he is still making (1668). But for many days after, Mr. Smith who had most wrestled with the Divell, was sore sick vomiting blood and having no rest at night until he prayed in this wise.'

'God pardon me. I will have no more discourse with Divells', at which he became well again.

"All this happened in the year 1665. The next year Mr. William Gates and the rest went to war in the South, I remaining at Johnabad to cast more guns for the wars. Mr. Gates was killed in the wars with Sivajee, and did afterwards make an appearance to me which I regarded not deeming it a wham (dream). So again, one night when I lay abed about 12 of the night, a Ghost came to my bed and gave me a great blow on the chest saying:

'Arise, Do you not know me?'

At this I was sore afraid and said: 'Get you gone in the name of the Father, the Son, and the Holy Ghost.'

Then said the Ghost: 'I am no Divell but William Gates that lieth dead at Bijapur. Rise you up and follow me or 'twill be the worse for you.'

'Though all the doors were locked yet we passed clear through them the Spirit going before, I following until we had gone about 200 yards. Then staying, it said:

'I have here buried some money and cannot rest until I shew you where it is, Guard you (take heed?)'

And with that he stamp't hard on the ground and so vanish't away. I fell down in a swoon awakening not until next morning at which time I found a stake in the ground at my head I made relation of what had passed to Mr. Smith, after which we both digged at that place and took up an earthen pot in which was much money, put there by Mr. Gates. This we sent to the poor of the parish of Stepmey wherein Mr. Gates was born, which must have pleased the Spirit, for it came no more. I would have kept the money for myself, but Mr. Smith advised otherwise.

In the year 1668, I John Cambell took leave from the Mogul and went on my travels wherein I had much wondrous adventure.

From Indian State Railways Magazine (April 1933)

The Men-Tigers
by Lt. Col. W.H. Sleeman

R AM CHUND ROO, COMMONLY CALLED THE SUREEMUNT, chief of Deoree, here overtook me. He came out from Saugor to visit me at Dhamoree, and not reaching that place in time came on after me. He held Deoree under the Peshwa, as the Saugor chief held Saugor, for the payment of the public establishments kept up for the local administration. It yielded him about ten thousand pounds a year, and when we took possession of the country he got an estate in the Saugor district, in rent-free tenure, estimated at fifteen hundred pounds a year. This is equal to about six thousand pounds a year in England. The tastes of native gentlemen lead them always to expend the greater part of their incomes in the wages of trains of followers of all descriptions, and in horses, elephants, & c.; and labour and the subsistence of labour are about four times cheaper in India than in England. By the breaking up of public establishments, and consequent diminution of the local demand for agricultural produce, the value of land throughout all central India, after the termination of the Mahratta war in 1817, fell by degrees thirty per cent.; and among the rest that of my poor friend the Sureemunt. While I had the civil charge of the Saugor district, in 1831, I represented this case of hardship; and government, in the spirit of liberality which has generally characterized their measures in this part of India, made up to him the difference between what he actually received and what they had intended to give him; and he has ever since felt grateful to me. He is a very small man, not more than five feet high; but he has the handsomest face I have almost ever seen; and his manners are those of the most perfect native gentleman. He came to call upon me after breakfast, and the conversation turned upon the number of people that had of late been killed by tigers between Saugor and Deoree, his ancient capital, which lies about midway between Saugor and the Nerbudda river. One of his followers, who stood behind his chair, said, "that when a tiger had killed one man he was safe, for the spirit of the man rode upon his head, and guided him from all danger. The spirit knew very well that the tiger would be watched for many days at the place where he had committed the homicide, and always guided him off to some other more secure place, where he killed other men without any risk to himself. He did not exactly know why the spirit of the man should thus befriend the beast that had killed him; but," added he, "there is a mischief inherent in spirits; and the better the man the more mischievous is his ghost, if means are not taken to put him to rest." This is the popular and general belief throughout India; and it is supposed, that the only sure mode of destroying a tiger, who has killed many people is, to begin by making offerings to the spirits of his victims, and thereby depriving him of their valuable services!* The belief that men are turned into tigers by eating of a root is no less general throughout India.

The Sureemunt, on being asked by me what he thought of the matter, observed, "there was no doubt much truth in what the man said; but he was himself of opinion, that the tigers which now infest the wood from Saugor to Deoree were of a different kind—in fact, that they were neither more nor less than men turned into tigers— a thing which took place in the woods of central India much more often than people were aware of. The only visible difference between the two," added the Sureemunt, "is that the metamorphosed tiger has *no tail*, while the *bora*, or ordinary tiger, has a very long one. In the jungle about Deoree," continued he, "there is a root which, if a man eat of, he is converted into a tiger on the spot; and if in this state he can eat of another, he becomes a man again—a melancholy instance of the former of which," said he, "occurred,

---

* When Agrippina, in her rage with her son Nero, threatens to take her step-son, Britannicus, to the camp of the Legion, and there assert his right to the throne, she invokes the spirit of his father, whom she had poisoned, and the manes of the Silani, whom she had murdered.

I am told, in my own father's family when I was an infant. His washerman, Rughoo, was, like all washermen, a great drunkard; and being seized with a violent desire to ascertain what a man felt in the state of a tiger, he went one day to the jungle and brought home two of these roots, and desired his wife to stand by with one of them, and the instant she saw him assume the tiger's shape, to thrust it into his mouth. She consented, the washerman ate his root, and became instantly a tiger; but his wife was so terrified at the sight of her old husband in this shape, that she ran off with the antidote in her hand. Poor old Rughoo took to the woods, and there ate a good many of his old friends from the neighbouring villages; but he was at last shot and recognized from the circumstance of his *having no tail*. You may be quite sure," concluded Sureemunt, "when you hear of a tiger without a tail, that it is some unfortunate man who has eaten of that root—and of all the tigers he will be found the most mischievous."

How my friend had satisfied himself of the truth of this story I know not, but he religiously believes it, and so do all his attendants and mine; and out of a population of thirty thousand people in the town of Saugor, not one would doubt the story of the washerman if he heard it.

I was one day talking with my friend, the Rajah of Myhere, on the road between Jubbulpore and Mirzapore, on the subject of the number of men who had been lately killed by tigers at the Kutra Pass on that road, and the best means of removing the danger. "Nothing," said the Rajah, "could be more easy or more cheap than the destruction of these tigers, if they were of ordinary sort;

but the tigers that kill men by wholesale, as these do, are, you may be sure, men themselves converted into tigers by the force of their *science*; and such animals are of all the most unmanageable."

"And how is it, Rajah Sahib, that these men convert themselves into tigers?"

"Nothing," said he, "is more easy than this to persons who have once acquired the science; but how they learn it, or what it is, we unlettered men know not. There was once a high priest, of a large temple, in this very valley of Myhere, who was in the habit of getting himself converted into a tiger by the force of this science, which he had thoroughly acquired. He had a necklace, which one of his disciples used to throw over his neck the moment the tiger's form became fully developed. He had, however, long given up the practice, and all his old disciples had gone off on their pilgrimages to distant shrines, when he was one day seized with a violent desire to take his old form of the tiger. He expressed the wish to one of his new disciples, and demanded whether he thought he might rely upon his courage to stand by and put on the necklace. 'Assuredly you may,' said the disciple; 'such is my faith in you, and in the God we serve, that I fear nothing!' The high priest upon this put the necklace into his hand with the requisite instructions, and forthwith began to change his form. The disciple stood trembling in every limb, till he heard him give a roar that shook the whole edifice, when he fell flat upon his face, and dropped the necklace on the floor. The tiger bounded over him, and out at the door; and infested all the roads leading to the temple for many years afterwards."

"Do you think, Rajah Sahib, that the old high priest is one of the tigers at the Kutra Pass?"

"No, I do not; but I think that they may be all men who have become imbued with a little too much of the high priest's *science*— when men once acquire this science they can't help exercising it, though it be to their own ruin and that of others."

"But, supposing them to be ordinary tigers, what is the simple plan you propose to put a stop to their depredations, Rajah Sahib?"

"I propose," said he, "to have the spirits that guide them propitiated by proper prayers and offerings; for the spirit of every man or woman who has been killed by a tiger rides upon his head, or runs before him, and tells him where to go to get prey, and to avoid danger. Get some of the Gonds, or wild people from the jungles, who are well skilled in these matters—give them ten or twenty rupees, and bid them go and raise a small shrine, and there sacrifice to these spirits. The Gonds will tell them that they shall, on this shrine, have regular worship, and good sacrifices of fowls, goats, and pigs, every year at least, if they will but relinquish their offices with the tigers and be quiet. If this is done, I pledge myself," said the Rajah, "that the tigers will soon get killed themselves, or cease from killing men. If they do not, you may be quite sure that they are not ordinary tigers, but men turned into tigers, or that the Gonds have appropriated all you gave them to their own use, instead of applying it to conciliate the spirits of the unfortunate people!"

From *Rambles and Recollections of
An Indian Official* by Lt. Col. W.H. Sleeman
of the Bengal Army, Vol I.

Haunted Villages

by Lt. Col. W.H. Sleeman

O N THE 16TH, WE CAME ON NINE MILES TO AMABAE, THE frontier village of the Jansee territory, bordering upon Duteea, where I had to receive the farewell visits of many members of the Jansee parties, who came on to have a quiet opportunity to assure me, that whatever may be the final order of the supreme government, they will do their best for the good of the people and the state, in whose welfare I feel great interest, for I have always considered Jansee among the native states of Bundelcund as a kind of oasis in the desert—the only one in which man can accumulate property with the confidence of being permitted by its rulers freely to display and enjoy it. I had also to receive the visit of messengers from the Rajah of Duteea, at whose capital we were to encamp the next day; and finally, to take leave of my amiable little friend the Sureemunt, who here left me on his return to Saugor, with a heavy heart I really believe.

We talked of the common belief among the agricultural classes, of villages being haunted by the spirits of ancient proprietors, whom it was thought necessary to propitiate. "He knew," he said, "many instances where these spirits were so very *froward*, that the present heads of the villages which they haunted, and the members of their little communities, found it almost impossible to keep them in good humour; and their cattle and children were, in consequence, always liable to serious accidents of one kind or another. Sometimes they were bitten by snakes, sometimes became possessed by devils; and at others, were thrown down and beaten most unmercifully." Any person who falls down in an epileptic fit, is supposed to be thrown down by a ghost, or possessed by a devil. They feel little of our mysterious dread of ghosts—a sound *drubbing* is what they dread from them; and he who hurts himself in one of these fits is considered to have got it. "As for himself, whenever he found any one of the villages upon his estate haunted by the spirit of an old patel, (village proprietor,) he always made a point of giving him a *neat little shrine*; and having it well endowed and attended, to keep him in good humour: this he thought was a duty that every landlord owed to his tenants!" Ramchund, the pundit, said, "That villages which had been held by old Gond (mountaineer) proprietors were more liable than any other to those kinds of visitations—that it was easy to say what village was and was not haunted; but often exceedingly difficult to discover to whom the ghost belonged! This once discovered, his nearest surviving relation was, of course, expected to take steps to put him to rest; but," said he, "it is wrong to suppose that the ghost of an old proprietor must be always doing mischief—he is often the best friend of the cultivators, and of the present proprietor, too, if he treats him with proper respect; for he will not allow the people of any other village to encroach upon their boundaries with impunity; and they will be saved all the expense and annoyance of a reference to the Adawlut (judicial tribunals) for the settlement of boundary disputes. It will not cost much to conciliate these spirits; and the money is generally well laid out!"

Several anecdotes were told me in illustration; and all that I could urge against the probability or possibility of such visitations appeared to them very inconclusive and unsatisfactory; they mentioned the case of the family of village proprietors in the Saugor district, who had for several generations, at every new settlement, insisted upon having the name of the spirit of the old proprietor of another tribe inserted in the lease instead of their own, and thereby secured his good graces on all occasions. Mr. Fraser had before mentioned this case to me. In August, 1834, while engaged in the settlement of the land revenue of the Saugor district for twenty years, he was about to deliver the lease of the estate made out in due form to the head of the family, a very honest and respectable old gentleman, when he asked him, respectfully, in whose name it had been made out? "In yours to be sure; have you renewed your lease for twenty years?" The old man, in a state of great alarm, begged him to have it altered immediately, or he and his family would all be destroyed—that the spirit of the ancient proprietor presided over the village community and its interests; and that all affairs of importance were transacted in his name. "He is," said the old man, "a very jealous spirit; and will not admit of any living man being considered, for a moment, as a proprietor or joint proprietor of the estate! It has been held by me and my ancestors immediately under government for many generations; but the lease deeds have always been made out in his name; and ours have been inserted merely as his managers, or bailiffs—were this good old rule, under which we have so long prospered, to be now infringed, we should all perish under his anger." Mr. Fraser found, upon inquiry, that this had really been the case; and, to relieve the old man and his family from their fears, he had the papers made out afresh, and the *ghost* inserted as the proprietor! The modes of flattering and propitiating these beings, natural and supernatural, who are supposed to have the power to do mischief, are endless.

While I was in charge of the district of Nursingpore, in the valley of the Nerbudda, in 1823, a cultivator of the village of Bedoo, about twelve miles distant from my court, was one day engaged in the cultivation of his field on the border of the village of Burkhara, which was supposed to be haunted by the spirit of an old proprietor, whose temper was so froward and violent that the lands could hardly be let for anything; for hardly any man would venture to cultivate them lest he might unintentionally incur his ghostship's displeasure. The poor cultivator, after begging his pardon in secret, ventured to drive his plough a few yards beyond the proper line of his boundary, and thus to add half an acre of the lands of Burkhara to his own little tenement, which was situated in Bedoo. That very night his only son was bitten by a snake, and his two bullocks were seized with the murrain. In terror he went off to the village temple, confessed his sin, and vowed not only to restore the half acre of land to the village of Burkhara, but to build a very handsome shrine upon the spot as a perpetual sign of his repentance. The boy and the bullocks all three recovered, and the shrine was built; and is, I believe, still to be seen as the boundary mark!

The fact was, that the village stood upon and elevated piece of ground rising out of a moist plain, and a colony of snakes had taken up their abode in it. The bites of these snakes had, on many occasions, proved fatal; and such accidents were all attributed to the anger of a spirit, which was supposed to haunt the village. At one time, under the former government, no one would take a lease of the village on any terms; and it had become almost entirely deserted, though the soil was the finest in the whole district. With a view to remove the whole prejudices of the people, the governor, Goroba Pundit, took the lease himself at the rent of one thousand rupees a year; and in the month of June went from his residence, twelve miles, with ten of his own ploughs, to superintend the commencement of so *perilous* an undertaking. On reaching the middle of the village, situated on the top of the little hill, he alighted from his horse, sat down upon a carpet that had been spread for him under a large and beautiful banyan tree, and began to refresh himself with a pipe before going to work in the fields.

As he quaffed his hookah, and railed at the follies of men, "whose absurd superstitions had made them desert so beautiful a village with so noble a tree in its centre," his eyes fell upon an enormous black snake which had coiled round one of its branches immediately over his head, and seemed as if resolved at once to pounce down and punish him for his blasphemy! He gave his pipe to his attendant, mounted his horse, from which the saddle had not yet been taken, and never pulled rein till he got home. Nothing could ever induce him to visit this village again, though he was afterwards employed under me as a native collector; and he has often told me, that he verily believed this was the spirit of the old landlord that he had unhappily neglected to propitiate before taking possession!

My predecessor in the civil charge of that district, the late Mr. Lindsay, of the Bengal civil service, again tried to remove the prejudices of the people against the occupation and cultivation of this fine village. It had never been measured; and all the revenue officers, backed by all the farmers and cultivators of the neighbourhood, declared that the spirit of the old proprietor would never allow it to be so. Mr. Lindsay was a good geometrician, and had long been in the habit of superintending his revenue surveys himself; and on this occasion he thought himself particularly called upon to do so. A new measuring cord was made for the occasion, and with fear and trembling all his officers attended him to the first field; but in measuring it the rope, by some accident, broke! Poor Lindsay was that morning taken ill, and obliged to return to Nursingpore, where he died soon after from fever. No man was ever more beloved by all classes of the people of his district than he was; and I believe there was not one person among them who did not believe him to have fallen a victim to the resentment of the spirit of the old proprietor. When I went to the village some years afterwards, the people in the neighbourhood all declared to me, that they saw the cord with which he was measuring, fly into a thousand pieces the moment the men attempted to straighten it over the first field.

A very respectable old gentleman from the Concan, or Malabar coast, told me one day, that every man there protects his field of corn and his fruit tree by dedicating it to one or other of the spirits which there abound, or confiding it to his guardianship. He sticks up something in the field, or ties on something to the tree, in the name of the said spirit, who from that moment feels himself responsible for its safe keeping. If any one, without permission from the proprietor, presumes to take either an ear of corn from the field, or fruit from the tree, he is sure to be killed outright or made extremely ill. "No other protection is required," said the old gentleman, "for our fields and fruit trees in that direction, though whole armies should have to march through them. I once saw a man come to the proprietor of a jack tree, embrace his feet, and in the most piteous manner implore his protection. He asked what was the matter. 'I took,' said the man, 'a jack from your tree yonder three days ago, as I passed at night; and I have been suffering dreadful agony in my stomach ever since. The spirit of the tree is upon me, and you only can pacify him.' The proprietor took up a bit of cow-dung, moistened it, and made a mark with it upon the man's forehead *in the name of the spirit*, and put some of it into the knot of hair on the top of his head. He had no sooner done this, than the man's pains all left him, and he went off, vowing never again to give similar cause of offence to one of these guardian spirits."

"Men," said my old friend, "do not die there in the same regulated spirit, with their thoughts directed exclusively towards God, as in other parts; and whether a man's spirit is to haunt the world or not after his death all depends on that."

From *Rambles and Recollections of An Indian Official* by Lt. Col. W.H. Sleeman of the Bengal Army, Vol I.

The Return of Imray

by Rudyard Kipling

IMRAY ACHIEVED THE IMPOSSIBLE. WITHOUT WARNING, FOR no conceivable motive, in his youth, at the threshold of his career, he chose to disappear from the world—which is to say, the little Indian station where he lived.

Upon a day he was alive, well, happy, and in great evidence among the billiard tables at his Club. Upon a morning he was not, and no manner of search could make sure where he might be. He had stepped out of his place; he had not appeared at his office at the proper time, and his dogcart was not upon the public roads. For these reasons, and because he was hampering, in a microscopical degree, the administration of the Indian Empire, that Empire paused for one microscopical moment to make inquiry into the fate of Imray. Ponds were dragged, wells were plumbed, telegrams were dispatched down the lines of railways and to the nearest seaport town—twelve hundred miles away; but Imray was not at the end of the drag-ropes nor the telegraph wires. He was gone, and his place knew him no more. Then the work of the great Indian Empire swept forward, because it could not be delayed, and Imray from being a man became a mystery—such a thing as men talk over at their tables in the Club for a month, and then forget utterly. His guns, horses, and carts were sold to the highest bidder. His superior officer wrote an altogether absurd letter to his mother, saying that Imray had unaccountably disappeared, and his bungalow stood empty.

After three or four months of the scorching hot weather had gone by, my friend Strickland, of the Police, saw fit to rent the bungalow from the native landlord. This was before he was engaged to Miss Youghal—an affair which has been described in another place—and while he was pursuing his investigations into native life. His own life was sufficiently peculiar, and men complained of his manners and customs. There was always food in his house, but there were no regular times for meals. He ate, standing up and walking about, whatever he might find at the sideboard, and this is not good for human beings. His domestic equipment was limited to six rifles, three shot-guns, five saddles, and a collection of stiff-jointed mahseer-rods, bigger and stronger than the largest salmon-rods. These occupied one-half of his bungalow, and the other half was given up to Strickland and his dog Tietjens—an enormous Rampur slut who devoured daily the rations of two men. She spoke to Strickland in a language of her own; and whenever, walking abroad, she saw things calculated to destroy the peace of Her Majesty the Queen-Empress, she returned to her master and laid information. Strickland would take steps at once, and the end of his labours was trouble and fine and imprisonment for other people. The natives believed that Tietjens was a familiar spirit, and treated her with the great reverence that is born of hate and fear. One room in the bungalow was set apart for her special use. She owned a bedstead, a blanket, and a drinking-trough, and if anyone came into Strickland's room at night her custom was to knock down the invader and give tongue till someone came with a light. Strickland owed his life to her when he was on the Frontier in search of a local murderer, who came in the grey dawn to send Strickland much farther than the Andaman Islands. Tietjens caught the man as he was crawling into Strickland's tent with a dagger between his teeth; and after his record of iniquity was established in the eyes of the law he was hanged. From that date Tietjens wore a collar of rough silver, and employed a monogram on her night blanket; and the blanket was of double woven Kashmir cloth, for she was a delicate dog.

Under no circumstances would she be separated from Strickland; and once, when he was ill with fever, made great trouble for the doctors, because she did not know how to help her master and would not allow another creature to attempt aid. Macarnaght, of the Indian Medical Service, beat her over her head with a gun-butt before she could understand that she must give room for those who could give quinine.

A short time after Strickland had taken Imray's bungalow, my business took me through that Station, and naturally, the Club quarters being full, I quartered myself upon Strickland. It was a desirable bungalow, eight-roomed and heavily thatched against any chance of leakage from rain. Under the pitch of the roof ran a ceiling-cloth which looked just as neat as a whitewashed ceiling. The landlord had repainted it when Strickland took the bungalow. Unless you knew how Indian bungalows were built you would never have suspected that above the cloth lay the dark three-cornered cavern of the roof, where the beams and the underside of the thatch harboured all manner of rats, bats, ants, and foul things.

Tietjens met me in the verandah with a bay like the boom of the bell of St Paul's, putting her paws on my shoulder to show she was glad to see me. Strickland had contrived to claw together a sort of meal which he called lunch, and immediately after it was finished went out about his business. I was left alone with Tietjens and my own affairs. The heat of the summer had broken up and turned to the warm damp of the rains. There was no motion in the heated air, but the rain fell like ramrods on the earth, and flung up a blue mist when it splashed back. The bamboo, and the custard apples, the poinsettias, and the mango trees in the garden stood still while the warm water lashed through them, and the frogs began to sing among the aloe hedges. A little before the light failed, and when the rain was at its worst, I sat in the back verandah and heard the water roar from the eaves, and scratched myself because I was covered with the thing called prickly heat. Tietjens came out with me and put her head in my lap and was very sorrowful; so I gave her biscuits when tea was ready, and I took tea in the back verandah on account of the little coolness found there. The rooms of the house were dark behind me. I could smell Strickland's saddlery and the oil on his guns, and I had no desire to sit among these things. My own servant came to me in the twilight, the muslin of his clothes clinging tightly to his drenched body, and told me that a gentleman had called and wished to see someone. Very much against my will, but only because of the darkness of the rooms, I went into the naked drawing-room, telling my man to bring the lights. There might or might not have been a caller waiting—it seemed to me that I saw a figure by one of the windows—but when the lights came there was nothing save the spikes of the rain without, and the smell of the drinking earth in my nostrils. I explained to my servant that he was no wiser than he ought to be, and went back to the verandah to talk to Tietjens. She had gone out into the wet, and I could hardly coax her back to me, even with biscuits with sugar tops. Strickland came home, dripping wet, just before dinner, and the first thing he said was:

'Has anyone called?'

I explained, with apologies, that my servant had summoned me into the drawing-room on a false alarm; or that some loafer had tried to call on Strickland, and thinking better of it, had fled after giving his name. Strickland ordered dinner, without comment, and since it was a real dinner with a white tablecloth attached, we sat down.

At nine o'clock Strickland wanted to go to bed, and I was tired too. Tietjens, who had been lying underneath the table, rose up, and swung into the least exposed verandah as soon as her master moved to his own room, which was next to the stately chamber set apart for Tietjens. If a mere wife had wished to sleep out of doors in that pelting rain it would not have mattered; but Tietjens was a dog, and therefore the better animal. I looked at Strickland, expecting to see him flay her with a whip. He smiled queerly, as a man would smile after telling some unpleasant domestic tragedy. 'She has done this ever since I moved in here,' said he. 'Let her go.'

The dog was Strickland's dog, so I said nothing, but I felt all that Strickland felt in being thus made light of. Tietjens encamped outside my bedroom window, and storm after storm came up, thundered on the thatch, and died away. The lightning spattered the sky as a thrown egg spatters a barn door, but the light was pale blue, not yellow; and, looking through my split bamboo blinds, I could see the great dog standing, not sleeping, in the verandah, the hackles alift on her back and her feet anchored as tensely as the drawn wire-rope of a suspension bridge. In the very short pauses of the thunder I tried to sleep, but it seemed that someone wanted me very urgently. He, whoever he was, was trying to call me by name, but his voice was no more than a husky whisper. The thunder ceased, and Tietjens went into the garden and howled at the low moon. Somebody tried to open my door, walked about and about through the house, and stood breathing heavily in the verandahs, and just when I was falling asleep I fancied that I heard a wild hammering and clamouring above my head or on the door.

I ran into Strickland's room and asked him whether he was ill, and had been calling me. He was lying on his bed half dressed, a pipe in his mouth. 'I thought you'd come,' he said. 'Have I been walking round the house recently?'

I explained that he had been tramping in the dining-room and the smoking-room and two or three other places, and he laughed and told me to go back to bed. I went back to bed and slept till the morning, but through all my mixed dreams I was sure I was doing someone an injustice in not attending to his wants. What those wants were I could not tell; but a fluttering, whispering, bolt-fumbling, lurking, loitering someone was reproaching me for my slackness, and, half awake, I heard the howling of Tietjens in the garden and the threshing of the rain.

I lived in that house for two days. Strickland went to his office daily, leaving me alone for eight or ten hours with Tietjens for my only companion. As long as the full light lasted I was comfortable, and so was Tietjens; but in the twilight she and I moved into the back verandah and cuddled each other for company. We were alone in the house, but none the less it was much too fully occupied by a tenant with whom I did not wish to interfere. I never saw him, but I could see the curtains between the rooms quivering where he had just passed through; I could hear the chairs creaking as the bamboos sprung under a weight that had just quitted them; and I could feel when I went to get a book from the dining-room that somebody was waiting in the shadows of the front verandah till I should have gone away. Tietjens made the twilight more interesting by glaring into the darkened rooms with every hair erect, and following the motions of something that I could not see. She never entered the rooms, but her eyes moved interestedly: that was quite sufficient. Only when my servant came to trim the lamps and make all light and habitable she would come in with me and spend her time sitting on her haunches, watching an invisible extra man as he moved about behind my shoulder. Dogs are cheerful companions.

I explained to Strickland, gently as might be, that I would go over to the Club and find for myself quarters there. I admired his hospitality, was pleased with his guns and rods, but I did not much care for his house and its atmosphere. He heard me out to the end, and then smiled very wearily, but without contempt, for he is a man who understands things. 'Stay on,' he said, 'and see what this thing means. All you have talked about I have known since I took the bungalow. Stay on and wait. Tietjens has left me. Are you going too?'

I had seen him through one little affair, connected with a heathen idol, that had brought me to the doors of a lunatic asylum, and I had no desire to help him through further experiences. He was a man to whom unpleasantness arrived as do dinners to ordinary people.

Therefore I explained more clearly than ever that I liked him immensely, and would be happy to see him in the daytime; but that I did not care to sleep under his roof. This was after dinner, when Tietjens had gone out to lie in the verandah.

'Pon my soul, I don't wonder,' said Strickland, with his eyes on the ceiling-cloth. 'Look at that!'

The tails of two brown snakes were hanging between the cloth and the cornice of the wall. They threw long shadows in the lamp-light.

'If you are afraid of snakes, of course —' said Strickland.

I hate and fear snakes, because if you look into the eyes of any snake you will see that it knows all and more of the mystery of man's fall, and that it feels all the contempt that the Devil felt when Adam was evicted from Eden. Besides which its bite is generally fatal, and it twists up trouser legs.

'You ought to get your thatch overhauled,' I said. 'Give me a mahseer-rod, and we'll poke 'em down.'

'They'll hide among the roof-beams,' said Strickland. 'I can't stand snakes overhead. I'm going up into the roof. If I shake 'em down, stand by with a cleaning-rod and break their backs.'

I was not anxious to assist Strickland in his work, but I took the cleaning-rod and waited in the dining-room, while Strickland brought a gardener's ladder from the verandah, and set it against the side of the room. The snake-tails drew themselves up and disappeared. We could hear the dry rushing scuttle of long bodies running over the baggy ceiling-cloth. Strickland took a lamp with him, while I tried to make clear to him the danger of hunting roof-snakes between a ceiling-cloth and a thatch, apart from the deterioration of property caused by ripping out ceiling-cloths.

'Nonsense!' said Strickland. 'They're sure to hide near the walls by the cloth. The bricks are too cold for 'em, and the heat of the room is just what they like.' He put his hand to the corner of the stuff and ripped it from the cornice. It gave with a great sound of tearing, and Strickland put his head through the opening into the dark of the angle of the roof-beams. I set my teeth and lifted the rod, for I had not the least knowledge of what might descend.

'H'm!' said Strickland, and his voice rolled and rumbled in the roof. 'There's room for another set of rooms up here, and, by Jove, someone is occupying 'em!'

'Snakes?' I said from below.

'No. It's a buffalo. Hand me up the two last joints of a mahseer-rod, and I'll prod it. It's lying on the main roof-beam.'

I handed up the rod.

'What a nest for owls and serpents! No wonder the snakes live here,' said Strickland, climbing farther into the roof. I could see his elbow thrusting with the rod. 'Come out of that, whoever you are! Heads below there! It's falling.'

I saw the ceiling-cloth nearly in the centre of the room sag with a shape that was pressing it downwards and downwards towards the lighted lamp on the table. I snatched the lamp out of danger and stood back. Then the cloth ripped out from the walls, tore, split, swayed, and shot down upon the table something that I dared not look at, till Strickland had slid down the ladder and was standing by my side.

He did not say much, being a man of few words; but he picked up the loose end of the tablecloth and threw it over the remnants on the table.

'It strikes me,' said he, putting down the lamp, 'our friend Imray has come back. Oh! you would, would you?'

There was a movement under the cloth, and a little snake wriggled out, to be back-broken by the butt of the mahseer-rod. I was sufficiently sick to make no remarks worth recording.

Strickland meditated, and helped himself to drinks. The arrangement under the cloth made no more signs of life.

'Is it Imray?' I said.

Strickland turned back the cloth for a moment, and looked. 'It is Imray,' he said; 'and his throat is cut from ear to ear.'

Then we spoke, both together and to ourselves: 'That's why he whispered about the house.'

Tietjens, in the garden, began to bay furiously. A little later her great nose heaved open the dining-room door.

She sniffed and was still. The tattered ceiling-cloth hung down almost to the level of the table, and there was hardly room to move away from the discovery.

Tietjens came in and sat down; her teeth bared under her lip and her forepaws planted. She looked at Strickland.

'It's a bad business, old lady,' said he. 'Men don't climb up into the roofs of their bungalows to die, and they don't fasten up the ceiling-cloth behind 'em. Let's think it out.'

'Let's think it out somewhere else,' I said.

'Excellent idea! Turn the lamps out. We'll get into my room.'

I did not turn the lamps out. I went into Strickland's room first, and allowed him to make the darkness. Then he followed me, and we lit tobacco and thought. Strickland thought. I smoked furiously, because I was afraid.

'Imray is back,' said Strickland. 'The question is—who killed Imray? Don't talk, I've a notion of my own. When I took this bungalow I took over most of Imray's servants. Imray was guileless and inoffensive, wasn't he?'

I agreed; though the heap under the cloth had looked neither one thing nor the other.

'If I call in all the servants they will stand fast in a crowd and lie like Aryans. What do you suggest?'

'Call 'em in one by one,' I said.

'They'll run away and give the news to all their fellows,' said Strickland.

'We must segregate 'em. Do you suppose your servant knows anything about it?'

He may, for aught I know; but I don't think it's likely. He has only been here two or three days,' I answered. 'What's your notion?'

'I can't quite tell. How the dickens did the man get the wrong side of the ceiling-cloth?'

There was a heavy coughing outside Strickland's bedroom door. This showed that Bahadur Khan, his body servant, had waked from sleep and wished to put Strickland to bed.

'Come in,' said Strickland. 'It's a very warm night, isn't it?'

Bahadur Khan, a great, green-turbaned, six-foot Mohammedan, said that it was a very warm night; but that there was more rain pending, which, by his Honour's favour, would bring relief to the country.

'It will be so, if God pleases,' said Strickland, tugging off his boots. 'It is in my mind, Bahadur Khan, that I have worked thee remorselessly for many days—ever since that time when thou first earnest into my service. What time was that?'

'Has the Heaven-born forgotten? It was when Imray Sahib went secretly to Europe without warning given; and I—even I—came into the honoured service of the protector of the poor.'

'And Imray Sahib went to Europe?'

'It is so said among those who were his servants.'

'And thou wilt take service with him when he returns?'

'Assuredly, Sahib. He was a good master, and cherished his dependants.'

'That is true. I am very tired, but I go buck-shooting tomorrow. Give me the little Sharp rifle that I use for black-buck; it is in the case yonder.'

The man stooped over the case; handed barrels, stock, and fore-end to Strickland, who fitted all together, yawning dolefully. Then he reached down to the gun-case, took a solid-drawn cartridge, and slipped it into the breech of the .360 Express.

'And Imray Sahib has gone to Europe secretly! That is very strange, Bahadur Khan, is it not?'

'What do I know of the ways of the white man, Heaven born?'

'Very little, truly. But thou shalt know more anon. It has reached me that Imray Sahib has returned from his so long journeyings, and that even now he lies in the next room, waiting his servant.'

'Sahib!'

The lamplights slid along the barrels of the rifle as they levelled themselves at Bahadur Khan's broad breast.

'Go and look!' said Strickland. 'Take a lamp. Thy master is tired, and he waits thee. Go!'

The man picked up a lamp, and went into the dining-room, Strickland following, and almost pushing him with the muzzle of the rifle. He looked for a moment at the black depths behind the ceiling-cloth; at the writhing snake under foot; and last, a grey glaze settling on his face, at the thing under the tablecloth.

'Hast thou seen?' said Strickland after a pause.

'I have seen. I am clay in the white man's hands. What does the Presence do?'

'Hang thee within the month. What else?'

'For killing him? Nay, Sahib, consider. Walking among us, his servants, he cast his eyes upon my child, who was four years old. Him he bewitched, and in ten days he died of the fever—my child!'

'What said Imray Sahib?'

He said he was a handsome child, and patted him on the head; wherefore my child died. Wherefore I killed Imray Sahib in the twilight, when he had come back from office, and was sleeping. Wherefore I dragged him up into the roof-beams and made all fast behind him. The Heaven-born knows all things. I am the servant of the Heaven-born.'

Strickland looked at me above the rifle, and said, in the vernacular, 'Thou art witness to this saying? He has killed.'

Bahadur Khan stood ashen grey in the light of the one lamp. The need for justification came upon him very swiftly. 'I am trapped,' he said, 'but the offence was that man's. He cast an evil eye upon my child, and I killed and hid him. Only such as are served by devils,' he glared at Tietjens, couched stolidly before him, 'only such could know what I did.'

'It was clever. But thou shouldst have lashed him to the beam with a rope. Now, thou thyself wilt hang by a rope. Orderly!'

A drowsy policeman answered Strickland's call. He was followed by another, and Tietjens sat wondrous still.

'Take him to the police station,' said Strickland. 'There is a case toward.'

'Do I hang, then?' said Bahadur Khan, making no attempt to escape, and keeping his eyes on the ground.

'If the sun shines or the water runs—yes!' said Strickland.

Bahadur Khan stepped back one long pace, quivered, and stood still. The two policemen waited further orders.

'Go!' said Strickland.

'Nay; but I go very swiftly,' said Bahadur Khan. 'Look! I am even now a dead man.'

He lifted his foot, and to the little toe there clung the head of the half-killed snake, firm fixed in the agony of death.

'I come of land-holding stock,' said Bahadur Khan, rocking where he stood. 'It were a disgrace to me to go to the public scaffold: therefore I take this way. Be it remembered that the Sahib's shirts are correctly enumerated, and that there is an extra piece of soap in his wash-basin. My child was bewitched, and I slew the wizard. Why should you seek to slay me with the rope? My honour is saved, and—and—I die.'

At the end of an hour he died, as they die who are bitten by a little brown *karait,* and the policemen bore him and the thing under the tablecloth to their appointed places. All were needed to make clear the disappearance of Imray.

'This,' said Strickland, very calmly, as he climbed into bed, 'is called the nineteenth century. Did you hear what the man said?'

'I heard,' I answered. 'Imray made a mistake.'

'Simply and solely through not knowing the nature of the Oriental, and the coincidence of a little seasonal fever. Bahadur Khan had been with him for four years.'

I shuddered. My own servant had been with me for exactly that length of time. When I went over to my own room I found my man waiting, impassive as the copper head on a penny, to pull off my boots.

'What has befallen Bahadur Khan' said I.

He was bitten by a snake and died. The rest the Sahib knows,' was the answer.

'And how much of this matter hast thou known?'

'As much as might be gathered from One coming in in the twilight to seek satisfaction. Gently, Sahib. Let me pull off those boots.'

I had just settled to the sleep of exhaustion when I heard Strickland shouting from his side of the house—

'Tietjens has come back to her place!'

And so she had. The great deerhound was couched statelily on her own bedstead on her own blanket, while, in the next room, the idle, empty ceiling-cloth waggled as it trailed on the table.

The Summoning of Arnold

by Alice Perrin

ONE OF THE MANY LESSONS THAT THE GREAT MOTHER India instils into the hearts of her white foster children is to sympathise with one another's troubles and misfortunes however trivial or however serious.

Therefore, when Mrs. Arnold, the Collector's wife at Usapore, was suddenly ordered home by the doctor, and Arnold could not get leave to go with her, it was sympathy with the husband's lonely unhappiness that made Williamson offer to move over to Arnold's bungalow and see him through the weary separation.

The offer was gratefully accepted, for the Arnolds had not been married long, and the man was missing his wife, and worrying about her ill-health to the verge of melancholia. So Williamson established himself in one half of the large, echoing bungalow, though there was no doubt that the move was somewhat inconvenient to himself! in fact, he admitted as much to me afterwards, when he was telling me of the horrible thing that happened while he was there.

But, being a thoroughly unselfish, good-hearted fellow, he thought little of his own inclinations and only endeavoured to prove a cheery companion, and help the other on from one English mail day to the other.

Arnold simply lived for the mail, and yet when his wife's letters did come he would be almost afraid to open them, in case she might be worse, or anything bad had happened. Williamson sometimes found it very difficult to keep his friend's spirits up to the mark, circumstances being unfavourable from every point of view. To begin with, Arnold himself was not in the best possible health, having had typhoid fever the previous year; he had the work of a large and turbulent district on his shoulders, no light burden; Usapore itself was a dismal, sandy little civil station; and, to crown it all, there seemed every prospect of the rains failing (which would mean a famine), and the heat was already beyond description.

However, the two men played mild tennis in the afternoons and whist in the baking little club in the evenings, and when they were alone they talked about Mrs. Arnold's last letter, and Arnold read bits of it aloud to Williamson, and always wound up by groaning over ' his infernal luck.'

'Why didn't I take leave six months ago when I could have got it?' he would reiterate; 'and then Lilla wouldn't have been ill, and

I should not have felt such a worm myself. But I hung on to escape the hot weather. I've never felt really fit since I had typhoid, and I believe it has played the dickens with my heart. And then this anxiety about Lilla is simply driving me mad. I'm in such a funk that she makes light of things not to worry me, and doesn't tell me what the doctors really say.'

But, in spite of these forebodings, Mrs. Arnold's letters continued to be very fairly satisfactory. She declared that she was better, that the air of Dover, where she was staying with her mother, was certainly doing her good, and the doctor hoped that in a few weeks she might be able to drop the *rôle* of invalid.

This sort of thing went on for several mails, and sometimes Arnold was in boisterous spirits, looking forward to his wife's return with the advent of the cold weather, while at others he plunged into the lowest depths of depression.

Then at last, one fatal evening, the English mail brought a letter from Mrs. Arnold saying that directly she could bear the move she was to go up to London to see a specialist. She besought her husband not to be anxious, the only reason for such a step being, she assured him, that the doctor thought she gained strength too slowly, and that, on the whole, it would be wiser to have the best advice.

Of course Arnold was in despair. That night, after eating no dinner, he sat outside on the plot of scorched grass in front of the house and surrendered himself to the gloomiest of views; and when bed-time came he refused to go in, saying he knew he should not sleep.

So Williamson lit another pipe and made up his mind to stay there too because it was the kind of night in India when, if a man is not happy, he probably begins to wander about the compound with a revolver to shoot pariah dogs that bark and keep him awake, and sometimes, instead of a dead dog, it is the man who is found shot, through the roof of his mouth. So Williamson watched Arnold very carefully, and tried to induce him to talk instead of sitting huddled up in his chair, with his hands hanging down at his sides.

'Buck up, old man!' he said encouragingly. 'If there'd been any bad news you would have had a telegram.'

'She may not have seen the London man yet,' replied Arnold. 'She said in her letter she thought it would be a fortnight before she could go.'

'Well, it's more than a fortnight since that letter was written. You look at the black side of things too much. Besides,' he added awkwardly, 'she wouldn't like it if she could see you now, Arnold. You know her one wish is that you shouldn't worry.'

Arnold straightened himself wearily.

'I know, I know,' he said, as if ashamed of his weakness. ' But when you care about a woman with all your heart and soul, Williamson, it's hell when you think there's any danger of losing her. Lilla is everything in the universe to me, and the parting from her was awful—our first parting! I wonder how a man manages to live out his life if his wife dies and he was really devoted to her—' He paused, and there was a dreamy silence, broken presently by the harsh scream of the brain fever bird rising to a desperate pitch and then subsiding.

'You'll laugh, perhaps, when I tell you,' he went on hesitatingly; 'but when she left me she said that if she died she would come straight to me first, and I gave her the same promise on my side. If anything happens to Lilla she will come herself and tell me. She will come and fetch me. I believe this with every atom of my being.'

❖

Williamson did not laugh. He felt a little cold thrill run down his back, and actually caught himself looking nervously over his shoulder. He was not a superstitious man by any means, but Arnold's voice sounded so unnatural; the surroundings looked so weird in the increasing light of the rising moon, which threw the long black shadow of a clump of bamboos across the dried-up patch of uneven grass; and the magnetic stillness in the thick, hot atmosphere was severed at intervals by the desperate cry of the brain fever bird, as it flew restlessly from tree to tree.

Williamson mentally called himself an ass. 'You'd better go to bed, Arnold,' he said bluntly; ' and if you apply for sick leave I'm sure you'd get it.'

Arnold laughed a little.

'Oh, I'm all right,' he said, 'and with a famine coming on I can't well ask for leave unless I'm actually too ill to work, which I'm not, and I don't think any doctor could honestly give me a certificate.'

Williamson thought otherwise, and determined to speak to the civil surgeon the next morning. In the meantime it was midnight, and if Arnold would only go to bed so much the better for them both.

'Come along,' he urged; 'you'll sleep all right if you go to bed now. The air will cool down very soon.'

They rose and went to their rooms, and shortly afterwards no sound was to be heard in the house or compound but the monotonous cry of the bird that would not rest.

Williamson undressed and threw himself on his bed. He listened at first to satisfy himself that Arnold was not moving about, and once he got up and crept to his friend's door, but there was only silence, so he went back to his room, and presently fell into an uneasy sleep.

An hour or two later he was suddenly awakened by the loud sound of a voice calling. He sat up, the echo of what he had heard still ringing in his ears : '*Lilla! Lilla!*' He could only conclude that Arnold had been shouting his wife's name in his sleep, so he waited a few moments, and the brain fever bird's discordant shriek rose and fell in the air. Perhaps that was what had disturbed him, the cry was not unlike the two syllables repeated over and over again.

He listened intently, and finally got up. He put on his slippers, and, taking his hand lamp, made his way to Arnold's open door. He did not speak, for if Arnold were asleep, it would never do to wake him, but he moved the curtain quietly to one side and looked into the room.

The punkah was swaying slowly to and fro, and Arnold was lying on his back, covered with a sheet. He seemed all right, but still Williamson was not quite satisfied. He carefully advanced, then stopped and looked apprehensively about him, sniffing the air, for it was full of a strong and unmistakable odour of chloroform.

The fear seized him that Arnold had committed suicide, and he hurried to the bedside. The smell of chloroform was overpowering, and, half choked with the fumes, he shouted at Arnold, and shook him desperately. There was no movement, no response. Faint and giddy, he rushed from the room, roused the servants and sent for the doctor, who, when he came, confirmed Williamson's fear, and said that Arnold was dead.

'Where is the bottle?' he said, when all restoratives had failed and hope was at an end.

'I couldn't see any bottle,' said Williamson, feeling as though he were in a nightmare. 'I looked, but I couldn't see anything. The smell was awful when I came into the room, and only a few minutes before I could have sworn I heard him shouting in his sleep. That was what woke me. It must have been hideously quick work.'

'It would have been,' said the doctor; 'his heart was so weak, it would not have taken very much to kill him.'

'Then you ought to have made him go on sick leave.'

'I suggested it when his ordinary leave was refused, but he said he wasn't bad enough, and I don't know that he was, if he had let himself alone. And then, with the prospect of a famine, a man can't conscientiously bolt unless he's in a hopeless way;' then, after a pause—'Had he a medicine chest anywhere?'

'I don't think so, but we'll look.' They looked, but found nothing, and they also questioned the punkah-coolie, who could give them no information beyond the fact that he had fallen asleep, and he thought the sahib had shouted to wake him.

So the doctor said it was one of those mysteries which would probably never be explained. Arnold had certainly killed himself with chloroform, but had taken some extraordinary precaution beforehand that the bottle should not be discovered.

But early next morning a telegram came from London for Arnold, which was opened by Williamson and the doctor. It told them that Mrs. Arnold had died while under chloroform, during an operation that had proved absolutely necessary.

'There !' cried Williamson, losing all self-control and beating his hands together like a maniac. ' That explains it! That's why there was no bottle—no trace of one! She came to fetch him—he said she would! He told me so only a few hours before. Oh! my God!'—and he sank into a chair, shuddering and shaking.

The doctor fetched some brandy.

'My dear fellow!' he said soothingly, 'pull yourself together. You're over-strung. Drink this and go and get some sleep, or I shall be sending you home on sick leave next.' Which he afterwards had to do, for Williamson was very ill, and for some weeks it was doubtful whether he would get over it. But he did recover, and was sent home, and just before he sailed he told me this story.

From *East of Suez* (1926)

Chunia, Ayah

by Alice Perrin

'I HOPE YOU CLEARLY UNDERSTAND THAT I DO NOT BELIEVE in ghosts?'

The little grey-haired spinster paused and regarded me with suspicion, and, alarmed lest I should, after all, lose the story I had been so carefully stalking, I vehemently reassured her on the point, whereupon, to my relief, she continued,—

'It certainly was a most extraordinary thing, and even now I hardly know what to make of it, though it happened a long time ago. One cold weather when I was in India keeping house for my brother, I received a letter from a friend, begging me to pay her a long-promised visit. She wrote that her husband was going into camp for a month to a part of his district where she could not accompany him, so that she and her little girl would be all alone, and I should be doing her a great kindness by coming. So the end of it was I accepted the invitation, though I greatly disliked leaving my brother to the tender mercies of the servants, and after a long, hot journey arrived at my destination at five o'clock one evening.

'My friend, Mrs. Pollock, was on the platform to meet me, and outside the station a bamboo cart was waiting, into which we climbed, and were soon bowling along the hard, white road at a brisk pace. Mary at once began to relate anecdotes of her little girl, whose name was Dot—how tall she was for her age (twenty months!), how much she ate, what she tried to say, what the ayah said about her, and so on.

'Now I must confess that I am not very fond of children; I like them well enough in their proper place (if that is not too near me), but I do not know how to behave towards them, and am always nervous as to what they will do or say next. Therefore, fond as I was of Mary herself, the subject of her conversation did not particularly interest me. When we arrived at the house, she actually inquired which I would do first—see Dot or have some tea! I boldly elected for tea, as I was exceedingly tired and thirsty, and I also reflected that if I did not at once make a determined stand, I should be Dot-ridden for the remainder of my visit.

'After tea I was taken to my room, and Mary brought her treasure to me for exhibition. She was the most lovely child I had ever beheld, with a grave, sweet face that quite won my unmotherly heart, and for once my prejudices completely melted away. Mary put her into my arms and stood by in an ecstacy of pride and delight as I proceeded to tap the pin-cushion, rattle my keys and perform various idiotic antics in my efforts to amuse Dot, who, I felt sure, would set up a howl in a few moments. But she watched my foolish attempts to be entertaining with an attentive gravity that was quite embarrassing, and charmed though I was with the little creature, I felt relieved when she held out her arms to go back to her mother.

'Mary called for the ayah to come and take the child to her nursery, and a woman with a sullen, handsome face entered and took her charge away. I remarked that the ayah looked bad-tempered, upon which Mary assured me that she could trust the child anywhere with her, and that she was a perfect treasure.

'The next morning I was awakened by a soft little pat on my face, and, opening my eyes, I found Dot holding herself upright by the corner, of my pillow.

'"Why, little one, are you all alone?" I said, lifting her on to the bed, and then I discovered that her feet were wringing wet.

'She held up one wet little foot and examined it carefully, and then pointed to the bathroom door, which was open, and from where I lay I could see an over-turned jug and streams of water on the floor—evidently Dot's handiwork. I put on my dressing-gown and took the child to her mother, explaining what had happened, and Mary hastily pulled off the soaking little shoes and socks and called for the ayah, who presently entered, and stood silently watching her mistress.

'"What do you mean by leaving the child in this way?" exclaimed Mary, angrily, and gathering up Dot's shoes and socks, she threw them to the ayah, bidding her bring others that were dry. One of the little shoes struck the woman on the cheek, for Mary was annoyed and had flung them with unnecessary force, and never shall I forget the look on the ayah's face as she left the room to carry out the order. It was the face of a devil, but Mary did not see it, for she was busy rubbing the cold little feet in her hands.

'"Mary," I said impulsively, "I am sure the ayah is a brute. Do get rid of her. I never saw anything so dreadful as the look she gave you just now."

'"My dear," answered Mary, with good-humoured impatience, "you have taken an unreasonable dislike to Chunia. She knew she was in the wrong and felt ashamed of herself."

'So the matter dropped; but I could not get over my dislike to Chunia, and as my visit wore on, and I became more and more attached to dear little Dot, I could hardly endure to see the child in her presence.

'My month with Mary passed quickly away, and I was really sorry when it was over, more especially as on my return home, my brother was called away unexpectedly on business, and I was left alone. I missed Dot more than I could have believed possible, for I had become ridiculously devoted to the small, round bundle of humanity, with the great dark eyes and short yellow curls, and my feelings are not to be described when the letter came from Mr. Pollock giving me the awful news of the child's death.

'I read the letter over and over again, hardly able to believe it. The whole thing was so hideously sudden! I had only left Mary and Dot such a short time ago, and when last I had seen the child she was in her mother's arms on the platform of the railway station, kissing her little fat hands laboriously to me in farewell, and looking the picture of life and health.

'Poor Mr. Pollock wrote in a heart-broken strain. It appeared that the child had strayed away one afternoon and must have fallen into the river, which ran past the bottom of the garden, for the little sun-hat was found floating in the stream, and close to the water's edge lay a toy that she had been playing with all day. Every search had been made, but no further trace could be found. The poor mother was distracted with sorrow, and Mr. Pollock had telegraphed for leave, as he meant to take her to England at once. He added that the ayah, Chunia, had been absent on three days leave when the dreadful accident happened, or, they both felt convinced, it would never have occurred at all. Mary, he wrote, sent me a message to beg me to take the woman into my service, as she could not endure the idea of one who had been so much with their darling going to strangers, for the poor woman had been a faithful servant, and was stricken and dumb with grief.

'I telegraphed at once that I would take Chunia willingly. I forgot my old antipathy to her, and only remembered that I should have someone about me who had known and loved the child so well. When the woman arrived I was quite shocked at her altered appearance. Her face seemed to have shrunk to half its former size, and her eyes looked enormous, and shone with a strange brilliancy. She was very quiet at first but burst into a flood of tears when I tried to speak to her of poor little Dot, so I gave it up, as I saw she could hardly bear the subject mentioned.

'She helped me to undress the first night, and then, instead of leaving the room, she stood looking at me without speaking.

'"What is it?" I inquired.

'" Mem-sahib," she said in a whisper, glancing over her shoulder, "may I sleep in your dressing-room to-night?"

'I willingly gave her permission, for I saw that the woman's nerves were unstrung and that she needed companionship. Then I got into bed, and must have been asleep for some hours when I awoke thinking I had heard a shrill voice crying in the compound. I listened, and again it came, a high, beseeching wail. It was certainly the voice of a child, and the awful pleading and despair expressed in the sound was heart-rending. I felt sure some native baby had wandered into the grounds and was calling hopelessly for its mother.

'I lit a candle and went into my dressing-room, where to my astonishment, I saw Chunia crouching against the outer door that led into the verandah, holding it fast with both hands as though she were shutting someone out.

'I asked what she was doing, and whether she knew whose child was crying outside. She sprang to her feet and answered sullenly that she had heard no child crying. I opened the door and went out into the verandah, but nothing was to be seen or heard, and I had no reply to my shouts of inquiry; so, concluding that it must have been my fancy, or perhaps some prowling animal, I returned to bed, and slept soundly for the rest of the night.

'The next evening I dined out, and on my return was surprised to hear someone talking in my dressing-room. I hurried in, and again found Chunia kneeling in front of the outer door imploring somebody to 'go away' at the top of her voice. Directly she saw me she came towards me excitedly.

'"Oh! mem-sahib!" she shrieked, "tell her to go away!"

'"Tell who?" I demanded.

'"Dottie-babba," she wailed, wringing her hands. "She cries to come to me—listen to her—listen!"

'She held her breath and waited, and I solemnly declare that as I stood and listened with her, I heard a child crying and moaning on the other side of the door. I was mute with horror and bewilderment, while the plaintive cry rose and fell, and then flinging the door open, I held the candle high above my head. There was no need of a light, for the moon was full, but no child could I see, and the verandah was quite empty. I determined to sift the matter to the bottom, so I went to the servants' quarters and called them all up. But no one could account for the crying of a child, and though the compound was thoroughly searched nothing was discovered. So the servants returned to their houses and I to my verandah, where I found Chunia in a most excited state.

'"Mem-sahib," she said, with her fists clenched and her eyes starting out of her head, "will she go away if I tell you all about it?"

'"Yes, yes," I cried soothingly, "tell me what you like."

'She silently took my wrist and dragged me into the dressing-room, shutting the door with the utmost caution.

'"Stand with your back against it," she whispered, "so that she cannot enter."

'I feared I was in the presence of a mad woman, so I did as she bade me, and waited quietly for her story. She walked up and down the room and began to speak in a kind of chant.

'"I did it," she sang. "I killed the child, little Dottie-babba, and she has followed me always. You heard her cry to-night and last night. The mem-sahib angered me the day she struck me with the shoe, and then a devil entered into my heart. I asked for leave, and went away, but it was too strong, it drew me back, and it said kill! kill! I fought and struggled against the voice, but it was useless. So on the second day of my leave I crept back and hid among the bushes till I saw the child alone, and then I took her away and killed her. She was so glad to see me, and laughed and talked, but when she saw the devil in my eyes she grew frightened, and cried just as you heard her cry to-night. I took her little white neck in my hands—see, mem-sahib, how large and strong my hands are—and I pressed and pressed until the child was dead, and then the devil left me. I looked and saw what I had done. I could not unclasp her fingers from my skirt, they clung so tightly, so I took it off and wrapped her in it—"

'The woman stopped suddenly. I had listened in silence, repressing the exclamations of horror that rose to my lips.

'"What did you do then?" I asked. Chunia looked wildly round.

'"I forget," she murmured; "the river, I ran quickly to the river—"

'Then there came a shriek from the dry, parched lips, and flinging her arms above her head she fell at my feet unconscious and foaming at the mouth.

'Afterwards Chunia was found to be raving mad, and the doctor expressed his opinion that she must have been in a more or less dangerous state for some months past. I told him of her terrible confession to me, but he said that possibly the whole thing was a delusion on her part.

'I went to see her once after she had been placed under restraint, but the sight was so saddening that I never went again. She was seated on the floor of her prison patting an imaginary baby to sleep, croning the quaint little lullaby that ayahs always use, and when I spoke to her she only gazed at me with dull, vacant eyes, and continued the monotonous chant as though she had not seen me at all.'

'And the child you heard crying?' I ventured to ask.

'Oh! How can I tell what it was? I don't know,' she answered with impatient perplexity. 'I can't believe that it was the spirit of little Dot, and yet—and yet— *what was it?*'

From *East of Suez* (1926)

Caulfield's Crime

by Alice Perrin

CAULFIELD WAS A SULKY, BAD-TEMPERED INDIVIDUAL WHO made no friends and was deservedly unpopular, but he had the reputation of being the finest shot in the Punjab, and of possessing a knowledge of sporting matters that was almost superhuman. He was an extremely jealous shot, and hardly ever invited a companion to join him on his shooting trips, so it may be understood that I was keenly alive to the honour conferred on me when he suddenly asked me to go out for three days' small game shooting with him.

'I know a string of jheels,' he said, 'about thirty miles from here, where the duck and snipe must swarm. I marked the place down when I was out last month, and I've made arrangements to go there next Friday morning. You can come, too, if you like.'

I readily accepted the ungracious invitation, though I could hardly account for it, knowing his solitary ways, except that he probably thought that I was unlikely to assert myself, being but a youngster, and also he knew me better than he did most people, for our houses were next door, and I often strolled over to examine his enormous collection of skins and horns and other sporting trophies.

I bragged about the coming expedition in the club that evening, and was well snubbed by two or three men who would have given anything to know the whereabouts of Caulfield's string of jheels, and who spitefully warned me to be careful that Caulfield did not end by shooting me.

'I believe he'd kill any chap who annoyed him,' said one of them, looking round to make sure that Caulfield was not at hand. 'I never met such a nasty-tempered fellow, I believe he's mad. But he can shoot, and what he doesn't know about game isn't worth knowing.'

Caulfield and I rode out the thirty miles early on the Friday morning, having sent our camp on ahead the previous night. We found our tents pitched in the scanty shade of some stunted dâk jungle trees with thick dry bark, flat, shapeless leaves, that clattered together when stirred by the wind, and wicked-looking red blossoms. It was not a cheerful spot, and the soil was largely mixed with salt which had worked its way in white patches to the surface, and only encouraged the growth of the rankest of grass.

Before us stretched a dreary outlook of shallow lake and swampy ground, broken by dark patches of reeds and little bushy islands, while on the left a miserable mud village overlooked the water. The sun had barely cleared away the thick, heavy mist, which was still slowly rising here and there, and the jheel birds were wading majestically in search of their breakfast of small fish, and uttering harsh, discordant cries.

To my astonishment, Caulfield seemed a changed man. He was in excellent spirits, his eyes were bright, and the sullen frown had gone from his forehead.

'Isn't it a lovely spot?' he said, laughing and rubbing his hands. 'Beyond that village the snipe ought to rise in thousands from the rice fields. We sha'n't be able to shoot it all in three days, worse luck, but we'll keep it dark, and come again. Let's have breakfast. I don't want to lose any time.'

Half an hour later we started, our guns over our shoulders, and a couple of servants behind us carrying the luncheon and cartridge bags. My spirits rose with Caulfield's, for I felt we had the certainty of an excellent day's sport before us.

But the birds were unaccountably wild and few and far between, and luck seemed dead against us. 'Some brutes' had evidently been there before us and harried the birds, was Caulfield's opinion, delivered with disappointed rage, and after tramping and wading all day, we returned, weary and crestfallen, with only a few couple of snipe and half a dozen teal between us. Caulfield was so angry he could hardly eat any dinner, and afterwards sat cursing his luck and the culprits who had forestalled us, till we could neither of us keep awake any longer.

The next morning we took a different route from the previous day, but with no better result. On and on, and round and round we tramped, with only an occasional shot here and there, and at last, long after midday, we sat wearily down to eat our luncheon. I was ravenously hungry, and greedily devoured my share of the provisions, but Caulfield hardly touched a mouthful, and only sat moodily examining his gun, and taking long pulls from his whisky flask. We were seated on the roots of a large tamarind tree, close to the village, and the place had a dreary, depressing appearance. The yellow mud walls were ruined and crumbling, and the inhabitants seemed scanty and poverty-stricken. Two ragged old women were squatting a short distance off, watching us with dim, apathetic eyes, and a few naked children were playing near them, while some bigger boys were driving two or three lean buffaloes towards the water.

Presently another figure came in sight—a fakir, or mendicant priest, as was evident by the tawny masses of wool woven amongst his own black locks and hanging in ropes below his shoulders, the ashes smeared over the almost naked body, and the hollow gourd for alms which he held in his hand. The man's face was long and thin, and his pointed teeth glistened in the sunlight as he demanded money in a dismal monotone. Caulfield flung a pebble at him and told him roughly to be off, with the result that the man slowly disappeared behind a clump of tall, feathery grass.

'Did you notice that brute's face?' said Caulfield as we rose to start again. 'He must have been a pariah dog in a former existence. He was exactly like one!'

'Or a jackal perhaps,' I answered carelessly. 'He looked more like a wild beast.'

Then we walked on, skirting the village and plunging into the damp, soft rice fields. We put up a wisp of snipe, which we followed till we had shot them nearly all, and then, to our joy, we heard a rush of wings overhead, and a lot of duck went down into the corner of a jheel in front of us.

'We've got 'em!' said Caulfield, and we hurried on till we were almost within shot of the birds, and could hear them calling to each other in their fancied security. But suddenly they rose again in wild confusion, and with loud cries of alarm were out of range in a second. Caulfield swore, and so did I, and our rage was increased ten-fold when the disturber of the birds appeared in sight, and proved to be the fakir who had paid us a visit at luncheon-time. Caulfield shook his fist at the man and abused him freely in Hindustani but without moving a muscle of his dog-like face the fakir passed us and continued on his way.

Words could not describe Caulfield's vexation.

'They were pin-tail, all of them,' he said, 'and the first decent chance we've had since we came out. To think of that beastly fakir spoiling the whole show, and I don't suppose he had the least idea what he had done.

'Probably not,' I replied, 'unless there was some spite in it because you threw a stone at him that time.'

'Well, come along,' said Caulfield, with resignation, 'we must make haste as it will be dark soon, and I want to try a place over by those palms before we knock off. We may as well let the servants go back as they've had a hard day. Have you got some cartridges in your pocket?'

'Yes, plenty,' I answered, and after despatching the two men back to the camp with what little game we had got, we walked on in silence.

The sun was sinking in a red ball and the air was heavy with damp, as the white mist stole slowly over the still, cold jheels. Far overhead came the first faint cackle of the wild geese returning home for the night, and presently as we approached the clump of palms we saw more water glistening between the rough stems, and on it, to our delight, a multitude of duck and teal.

But the next moment there was a whir-r-r of wings like the rumble of thunder, and a dense mass of birds flew straight into the air and wheeled bodily away, while the sharp, cold atmosphere resounded with their startled cries. Caulfield said nothing, but he set his jaw and walked rapidly forward, while I followed. We skirted the group of palms, and on the other side we came upon our friend the fakir, who had again succeeded in spoiling our sport. The long, lanky figure was drawn to its full height, the white eyeballs and jagged teeth caught the red glint of the setting sun, and he waved his hand triumphantly in the direction of the vanishing cloud of birds.

Then there came the loud report of a gun, and the next thing I saw was a quivering body on the ground, and wild eyes staring open in the agony of death. Caulfield had shot the fakir, and now he stood looking down at what he had done, while I knelt beside the body and tried hopelessly to persuade myself that life was not extinct. When I got up we gazed at each other for a moment in silence.

'What are we to do?' I asked presently.

'Well, you know what it means,' Caulfield said in a queer, hard voice. 'Killing a native is no joke in these days, and I should come out of it pretty badly.'

I glanced at the body in horror. The face was rigid, and seemed more beast-like than ever. I looked at Caulfield again before I spoke, hesitatingly.

'Of course the whole thing was unpremeditated—an accident.'

'No, it wasn't,' he said defiantly, 'I meant to shoot the brute, and it served him right. And you can't say anything else if it comes out. But I don't see why anyone should know about it but ourselves.'

'It's nasty business,' I said, my heart sinking at the suggestion of concealment.

'It will be nastier still if we don't keep it dark, and you won't like having to give me away, you know. Either we must bury the thing here and say nothing about it, or else we must take it back to the station and stand the devil's own fuss. Probably I shall be kicked out of the service.'

'Of course I'll stand by you,' I said with an effort, 'but we can't do anything this minute. We'd better hide it in that long grass and come back after dinner. We must have something to dig with.'

Caulfield agreed sullenly, and between us we pushed the body in amongst the thick, coarse grass, which completely concealed it, and then made our way back to the camp. We ordered dinner and pretended to eat it, after which we sat for half an hour smoking, until the plates were cleared away and the servants had left the tent. Then I put my hunting-knife into my pocket, and Caulfield picked up a kitchen chopper that his bearer had left lying on the floor, after hammering a stiff joint of a camp chair, and we quitted the tent casually as though intending to have a stroll in the moonlight, which was almost as bright as day. We walked slowly at first, gradually increasing our pace as we left the camp behind us, and Caulfield never spoke a word until we came close to the tall grass that hid the fakir's body. Then he suddenly clutched my arm.

'God in heaven!' he whispered, pointing ahead, 'what is that?'

I saw the grass moving, and heard a scraping sound that made my heart stand still. We moved forward in desperation and parted the grass with our hands. A large jackal was lying on the fakir's body, grinning and snarling at being disturbed over his hideous meal.

'Drive it away,' said Caulfield, hoarsely. But the brute refused to move, and as it lay there showing its teeth, its face reminded me horribly of the wretched man dead beneath its feet. I turned sick and faint, so Caulfield shouted and shook the grass and threw clods of soil at the animal, which rose at last and slunk slowly away. It was an unusually large jackal, more like a wolf, and had lost one of its ears. The coat was rough, and mangy and thickly sprinkled with grey.

For more than an hour we worked desperately with the chopper and hunting-knife, being greatly aided in our task by a rift in the ground where the soil had been softened by water running from the jheel, and finally we stood up with the sweat pouring from our faces, and stamped down the earth which now covered all traces of Caulfield's crime. We had filled the grave with some large stones that were lying about (remnants of some ancient temple, long ago deserted and forgotten), thus feeling secure that it could not easily be disturbed by animals.

The next morning we returned to the station, and Caulfield shut himself up more than ever. He entirely dropped his shooting, which before had been his one pleasure, and the only person he ever spoke to, unofficially, was myself.

The end of April came with its plague of insects and scorching winds. The hours grew long and weary with the heat, and dust storms howled and swirled over the station, bringing perhaps a few tantalising drops of rain, of more often leaving the air thick with a copper-coloured haze.

One night when it was too hot to sleep, Caulfield suddenly appeared in my verandah and asked me to let him stay the night in my bungalow.

'I know I'm an ass,' he said in awkward apology, 'but I can't stay by myself. I get all sorts of beastly ideas.'

I asked no questions, but gave him a cheroot and tried to cheer him up, telling him scraps of gossip, and encouraging him to talk, when a sound outside made us both start. It proved to be only the weird, plaintive cry of a jackal, but Caulfield sprang to his feet, shaking all over.

'There it is again!' he exclaimed. 'It has followed me over here. Listen!' turning his haggard, sleepless eyes on me. 'Every night that brute comes and howls round my house, and I tell you, on my oath, it's the same jackal we saw eating the poor devil I shot.'

'Nonsense, my dear chap,' I said, pushing him back into the chair, 'you must have got fever. Jackals come and howl round my house all night. That's nothing.'

'Look here,' said Caulfield, very calmly, 'I have no more fever than you have, and if you imagine I am delirious you are mistaken.' He lowered his voice. 'I looked out one night and saw the brute. It had only one ear!'

In spite of my own common sense and the certainty that Caulfield was not himself, my blood ran cold, and after I had succeeded in quieting him and he had dropped off to sleep on the couch, I sat in my long chair for hours, going over in my mind every detail of that horrible night in the jungle.

Several times after this Caulfield came to me and repeated the same tale. He swore he was being haunted by the jackal we had driven away from the fakir's body, and finally took it into his head that the spirit of the murdered man had entered the animal and was bent on obtaining vengeance.

Then he suddenly ceased coming over to me, and when I went to see him he would hardly speak, and only seemed anxious to get rid of me. I urged him to take leave or see a doctor, but he angrily refused to do either, and said he wished I would keep away from him altogether. So I left him alone for a couple of days, but on the third evening my conscience pricked me for having neglected him, and I was preparing to go over to his bungalow, when his bearer rushed in with a face of terror and besought me to come without delay. He said he feared his master was dying, and he had already sent for the doctor. The latter arrived in Caulfield's verandah simultaneously with myself, and together we entered the sick man's room. Caulfield was lying unconscious on his bed.

'He had a sort of fit, sahib,' said the frightened bearer, and proceeded to explain how his master had behaved.

The doctor bent over the bed.

'Do you happen to know if he had been bitten by a dog lately?' he asked, looking up at me.

'Not to my knowledge,' I answered, while the faint wail of a jackal out across the plain struck a chill to my heart.

For twenty-four hours we stayed with Caulfield, watching the terrible struggles we were powerless to relieve, and which lasted till the end came. He was never able to speak after the first paroxysm, which had occurred before we arrived, so we could not learn from him whether he had been bitten or not, neither could the doctor discover any scar on his body which might have been made by the teeth of an animal. Yet there was no shadow of doubt that Caulfield's death was due to hydrophobia.

As we stood in the next room when all was over, drinking the dead man's whisky and soda, which we badly needed, we questioned the bearer closely, but he could tell us little or nothing. His master, he said, did not keep dogs, nor had the bearer ever heard of his having been bitten by one; but there had been a mad jackal about the place nearly three weeks ago which his master had tried to shoot but failed.

'It couldn't have been that,' said the doctor; 'he would have come to me if he had been bitten by a jackal.'

'No,' I answered mechanically, 'it could not have been that.' And I went into the bedroom to take a last look at poor Caulfield's thin, white face with its ghastly, hunted expression, for there was now nothing more that I could do for him.

Then I picked up a lantern and stepped out into the dark verandah, intending to go home. As I did so, something came silently round the corner of the house and stood in my path. I raised my lantern and caught a glimpse of a mass of grey fur, two fiery yellow eyes, and bared, glistening teeth. It was only a stray jackal, and I struck at it with my stick, but instead of running away it slipped past me and entered Caulfield's room. The light fell on the animal's head, and I saw that it had only one ear.

In a frenzy I rushed back into the house calling for the doctor and servants.

'I saw a jackal come in here,' I said, searching round the bedroom, 'hunt it out at once.'

Every nook and corner was examined, but no jackal was found.

'Go home to bed, my boy, and keep quiet till I come and see you in the morning,' said the doctor, looking at me keenly. 'This business has shaken your nerves, and you imagination is beginning to play you tricks. Good-night.'

'Good-night,' I answered, and went slowly back to my bungalow, trying to persuade myself that he was right.

From *East of Suez* (1926)

A Ghost in Burma
(A Story Based on Fact)
by Gerald T. Tait

I**T IS A REMARKABLE FACT THAT GOOD FOOD AND DRINK SEEM** to have the power of stimulating the mind and memory, and in consequence, some of the best stories, whether they belong to the humorous series or whether they be yarns, are told after dinner. The following was no exception to the rule and we heard it at a friendly gathering of exiles on leave, united after many years of absence and many years of wandering in strange lands. Peter Kane, burnt mahogany by the tropical sun, tall, broad shouldered, who had spent the greater part of his service in wild corners of the Empire, had been listening for some time with a smile on his face, to a discussion on ghosts. Finally he broke into the conversation.

"Would you fellows like a true yarn on ghosts?" We naturally all assented. I have set it down in his own words and you may or may not believe it according to the amount of imagination or superstition, call it whatever you like, in your make up. As far as we were concerned, knowing Peter we believed the story.

"It happened years ago. I was only a young railway engineer then just out from Home. Ever since my early childhood the name "Burma" was magic to my mind; it typified all that represents the mysterious East, and you can imagine my joy on learning that I was appointed to that country of my dreams. My luck as I believed then was in the ascendant, for on my arrival, I found I was to join a survey party working towards the Chinese border lying beyond the river Salween. What more could a youngster wish for? A wild country, inhabited by few but very wild tribes, plenty of work, plenty of sport, and before us the unknown, the unexplored. As one grows older and more settled, I must confess one's ideas of luck differ somewhat and nowadays, luck to my mind is to get nearer home. However, for a youngster the outlook was ideal. I landed in Rangoon late in October and made my way by rail to Mandalay whence the survey expedition was to set forth. I can hardly describe the joy it was to me to see this country; I literally drank it all in and asked for more. From the very start, Rangoon with the great Shwe Dagon covered with gold, the multi-coloured crowd around its base, the orange robed priests, the pilgrims, the vendors, the beggars, crowded my brain with one confused mass of colour. Then in the train, I seemed to spend my time moving from one side of the carriage to the other. Everything struck me as picturesque, the paddy fields with those solemn white or gray paddy birds picking their way daintily through the slush, the smiling Burmans up to their knees in mud planting out the rice, little thatched roofed huts clustering around groves of great darkleaved trees, the whole country green and fertile.... So much for childish enthusiasm.

My stay in Mandalay was short; indeed we left two days after my arrival. The party consisted of Paddy Greene as Chief, a short, plump, cheery, fairhaired Irishman with always a twinkle in his eye, an amazing brogue and a divine voice when he sang. Then Tom Inglis, neither handsome nor ugly, just average looking exactly alike the hundreds of thousands of other men of the same class who have followed the same footsteps through Public School and University; entirely dependable and sound, never rattled. Next followed John Alaistairs, dark haired and morose; and lastly myself just a raw youngster without any particular distinction. The remainder of our staff consisted of native surveyors and a full complement of ubiquitous coolies.

The first portion of our journey was by train to railhead, situated about 100 to 150 miles from the Chinese frontier as the crow flies. In actual fact for us, this distance was just about double; for the country to be surveyed was extremely hilly and covered with dense and impenetrable jungle. The only existing trade routes being tracks following the crests of the ridges rising anything up to 5,000 feet above the bottom of the valleys. These tracks, however, were not for us. The road we had to travel followed not the ridges but the valleys and the slopes slightly above them. Those who have visited this part of the world and strayed from the beaten track, will readily understand what I mean when I talk about impenetrable jungle. Imagine a solid barrier of trees rising to 120 feet, covered with thick foliage close planted, with between them colossal bushes with thorns three or more inches long and clumps of thick bamboo; the whole woven into a solid mass by myriads of creepers, some with stems like a ship's hawser, the only relief from the monotonous green being patches of brightly coloured orchids; slopes amazingly steep and studded with rocks and boulders hidden by the undergrowth but more than noticeable when stumbled upon. Advance through this country meant about two miles a day with luck, every foot of path hewn by the axes of the special jungle-clearing coolies, and every foot stubbornly contested by the forest. To crown everything a dim semi-religious light filtered by the dark mantle of leaves overhead. Observations could only be made by laboriously climbing tall trees. A heartbreaking country but possessing an undeniable thrill in spite of the damp heat and the mosquitoes.

I must confess that at times I felt depressed and had it not been for Paddy and his tonic-like nature, I really don't know how we would have carried on. Alaistairs was more than a wet blanket and would alone have depressed a regiment. Inglis on the other hand seemed utterly undisturbed by his surroundings and might just as well have been walking down Piccadilly for all the effect they had on him.

You may think that I am drawing out this description unduly. I do it, however, with a purpose so that you will more fully grasp the inexplicableness of the subsequent find and events.

Our work went on and we crept further and further into the unknown depths towards the Salween. Finally after about two and a half months we stepped out on to the crest of a ridge almost devoid of trees, overlooking the surrounding country and in particular the Salween itself. The change from the monotony of our foregoing road to this open and wildly beautiful vista, swept away all feelings of depression.

We have now reached the setting for our drama. I will describe it so that you fellows may picture it in your minds.

The river flows with a rushing roar at the foot of immense perpendicular rocky walls forming a deep trench varying from 90 to 400 feet across. The bed of the river consists in a series of steps anything up to a mile long with a drop of ten or fifteen feet between each, turning the swift waters, sometimes into cascades, sometimes into rapids filled with boulders. The sides of this trench rise up to 1,000 or 1,500 feet above the level of the river. From the top the ground, covered with enormous rocks piled up into confused masses, stretches inland a few miles but rises to 5,000 and 6,000 feet, thus forming a valley about eight miles across with slopes set at 60 degrees. This valley receives numerous tributary streams, most of them contained in deep gorges cutting the main valley at right angles. The whole country is covered with dense jungle and tall rough grass. The few flat spaces to be seen are small golden sand banks on the edges of the side streams where, throughout the day, myriads of butterflies of every size and colour, dance and scintillate. Also here and there, small plateaux just above the level of the waters of the main stream, where the trench shallows and where the mantle of vegetation has slightly retreated. It is here, by the way, that are sometimes to be found the temporary shelters put up by the nomadic tribes of this country Moi, Khas and Tac-Cui, strayed from the neighbouring wilds of Laos. These patches show up brilliant emerald due to the wild plantains and the wild paddy thereon.

Through this decor of savage beauty we made our way to the banks of the river.

Two days were wasted looking for a place to cross.

The third morning on turning a bend, we suddenly came upon an amazing sight. On the opposite bank, perched upon an almost overhanging rock, stood a square bungalow, for all the world like the ordinary P.W.D. rest-houses found throughout India and Burma. We could hardly believe our eyes. The strangeness of this find in the middle of this dense jungle defied words. Our native followers themselves, we could see, were just as surprised as ourselves. One fact stood out very clearly. We had to examine this bungalow. A place was found, about half a mile down stream where the river was fordable and we finally reached the bungalow by two in the afternoon.

The East is a curious part of the world particularly in respect to the propagation of news and messages generally. Now remember our coolies had never been anywhere near this part of Burma before, nor had they ever heard of this bungalow; further, for weeks we had not seen any local natives. Yet one and all refused to approach saying that it was haunted. I asked them how they knew and the only reply I could obtain was "We have just been warned not to stay here." They were very insistent that it was not their fault, but how could they act against direct orders. As to "Who" gave the orders they would not say. No amount of questioning elucidated a further reply and finally they remained sullen and dumb.

This was most annoying for the idea of resting once more in civilised surroundings appealed to us tremendously. After a short discussion we decided to remain on the spot for three days provided of course we succeeded in propitiating our coolies. Before going any further, let me describe the general lay-out of the building.

Square, perched on a bare rock overlooking the Salween, it had a verandah running around on the three sides to landwards. The fourth side, an absolutely flat wall with just one window in the centre, overhung a 1,000-foot drop straight into the river below. In the very middle of the whole building, was an open courtyard with a large brick cube in the centre about 10 feet aside. The bungalow was in a fair state of repair yet unoccupied.

We were all as keen as mustard to investigate and entered, led by Paddy. In spite of our coolies' fears it seemed a very ordinary kind of habitation. The only odd thing about it was the brick cube in the courtyard and this particularly attracted Paddy's attention. For the time being, however, he said nothing and would pass no opinion as to its *raison d'etre*. Try as we would we could not evolve a theory as to how this building had been erected and by whom. We settled on our various rooms, Paddy, Inglis and myself chosing the room overlooking the river; Alaistairs preferring to be alone in a room off the courtyard. I could scarcely tear myself away from our window for the view was really magnificent with its sheer drop of a thousand feet into the roaring torrent below.

It took a good deal of persuasion to induce the coolies to carry our stores indoors and they only finally agreed to do so on the understanding that they would be allowed to sleep outside in the open glade roughly 300 feet across separating the building from the jungle. The joy of a rest in the cool verandahs with a sight of the blue sky above soon made us forget the fatigue of the journey. It was only towards evening that we once more began to take notice of our immediate surroundings. Paddy was the first to break the silence. "That brick cube in the courtyard puzzles me," he said, "I cannot for the life of me imagine what it was for." "I should say it was put up by the owner to hide a well," I suggested hopefully.

"Don't be an ass," he replied. "You may not believe me but that cube, unless I am very much mistaken, dates back some 5,000 years before the bungalow was ever built."

To say we were astonished is to say the least of it. We all sat up, thinking he was pulling our legs. Inglis, however, took the statement quite calmly. "How do you make that out?" he asked. Paddy replied:– "Being an engineer, the subject of building and building materials throughout the ages has always been of particular interest to me. Did any of you closely examine that cube? I think not. If you do you will find that its walls are built of plano-convex bricks, not made in moulds but fashioned by the hands of the maker on a flat surface, the top being left convex. This I may say is an absolute characteristic of the oldest Sumerian periods dating back to about 3,000 B.C. Remains of similar workmanship have been found in Mesopotamia at Kish and in India at Mohenjo-Daro. Furthermore, if you look at the surface you will see on some of the bricks curious small regular carvings which are nothing else but cuneiform writing. Unfortunately I cannot read it. This find would be of extraordinary interest to archæologists, if ever they believed us."

With one accord we rose and made for the courtyard. Paddy proceeded to explain the find to us on the spot. It undoubtedly tallied with all he said. Here then was yet another mystery.

Conversation at dinner that night consisted mainly in a lecture by Paddy and in theorising by the rest of us, needless to say, without any tangible results. We finally turned in at about ten and settled down to a good night's rest.

As far as I am concerned I fell asleep as soon as my head touched my pillow and I slept without a break until suddenly awakened by an unearthly shriek. It took me a minute before I came sufficiently to my senses to realise that it was not a dream. I jumped up to find Paddy and Inglis groping for their torches.

"What on earth was that," I cried.

"It seemed to come from Alaistair's room," replied Inglis, as we set off at a run. We found Alaistairs sitting up in bed. He apologised on seeing us saying that he had had a nightmare and dreamt that cold hands were grasping his neck. On being assured that he was safe we trooped back to bed again laughing at the alarm. The next day passed quickly and uneventfully. Alaistairs seemed quite cheerful for a change and pooh-poohed the idea of changing rooms.

Paddy spent the most of his time in examining his precious brick cube and making sketches of it. Night set in with its usual tropical rapidity and once more we settled down to sleep. This time I must confess the memory of Alaistairs' shriek kept me awake. I tried hard to sleep but without success; finally I could not stand it any longer and got up and went to the window in hopes of getting in little fresh air. The moon was not quite full but its light was sufficiently strong to show up the country for miles. Far below the sound of the rushing of water rose, here a woodpecker tapped unceasingly, there a night-jar or screech-owl disturbed by some jungle beast raised its voice in protest. I stretched my arms out and breathed deeply.

Now I want you particularly to note my position. I was standing leaning out of the window with only plain whitewashed perfectly flat walls without many crevice or ledge, stretching above, on both sides and below, where even a lizard would have had difficulty in finding purchase, while all round me was the gaping void of the precipice.

There I was breathing deeply when to my horror I felt my arms grasped by two cold and clammy invisible hands, coming apparently from straight in front of me. I let out an appalling yell. Inglis and Paddy jumped out of bed.

"For God's sake come," I shouted, "Something has got hold of me."

Inglis was the first to reach me. He caught hold of my arms and said "Hold on old man, I'll help you." His fingers crept up my extended arms. "Paddy, he is right, I can feel a hand."

My hair stood on end for nothing could be seen. "Catch hold of him," said Paddy who by this time had joined us, "and we'll pull together."

Their united effort was successful, the cold hands gradually slipped and then let go. I was once more free, unhurt but mighty scared. Paddy fetched some brandy and then examined the walls, but without success for it was a physical impossibility for any human being or even a monkey to hang on to that smooth surface. Having sufficiently recovered Paddy suggested looking up Alaistairs. We entered his room but to our surprise found it empty. Inglis was the first to make the discovery. Poor Alaistairs lay face downwards on the top of the cube, dead; his throat, showing the distinct markings of two hands. Dawn soon came. We organised a very complete search but it revealed nothing, not so much even as footprints in the dust on the top of the cube.

That is my story."

There was a short silence among us. Then someone asked: "What about the Sumerian cube, did you report it to anyone?"

Peter Kane gave a short laugh, "My dear fellow no one believed us; even Paddy's sketches were declared fakes. As for poor Alaistairs, we reported him as having died from fever contracted on the way out. You see, supernatural deaths are not popular with the powers that be."

Had the Sumerian cube anything to do with his death? Was it by chance an ancient sacrificial altar? How came the bungalow at that spot?—are questions yet to be answered.

From *Indian State Railway Magazine* (December 1928)

'There are more things—'
A Tale of the Malabar Jungles
by H.W. Dennys

IT WAS DORA TORRINGTON WHO STARTED THE SUBJECT AS WE lay in deck chairs near the tennis court enjoying that pleasant hour in late summer between sunset and the dressing gong. She was of the restless, wealthy type who are never happy unless mixed up in the very latest craze. It had started with Women Suffrage, and now consisted of a mania for a religion which, from her conversation, we gathered was a cross between Spiritualism and Christian Science. Her position as hostess gave her privileges, and her audience tried not to appear bored as she dwelt on a lecture she had recently attended.

"He was such a dear little man," she rambled, "all bald-head and forehead, and he gave us *such* an interesting talk on the subject of 'Faith.' Do you know he said that the Bible was quite correct,— literally I mean—when it says that faith can remove mountains, and he gave us all kinds of weird stories to prove what he said. Then he went on to say that he saw no reason why, if we had sufficient faith, we shouldn't be able to do even more than that, and actually *create* things! Wouldn't it be too thrilling if we could think of wanting a new car so hard that it suddenly arrived."

Her audience stirred. The idea had possibilities.

"Think too," said Vera, whom I would have you know is my wife, "of being able to concentrate so hard on Tim that half his face suddenly disappeared behind a beard. It might make him look quite distinguished, though I'm afraid," she added sadly, "it could never make him good-looking."

I stiffened. Humour of this type struck me as being crude and certainly unjust. I was about to launch a snappy counter-attack, when a grunt from the chair on my left diverted my attention.

Peter Mainwaring, who occupied it, was apparently the only one present who hadn't treated the idea as a joke, and as I glanced at him was mumbling to himself with a far away look in his, eyes.

I postponed my snappy reply, and gave him a dig with my elbow to bring him back to earth.

"What's biting you, Peter?" I enquired. "Bring it out and let the public enjoy it."

"It's not so foolish or impossible as you all think, because I've seen it," was the unexpected reply.

Ten pairs of eyes focussed themselves on Peter curiously, who finding himself the centre of attention, grew flurried and evidently regretted his remark.

"I scent a story," quoth pretty Yvonne Elder, removing her graceful young self from the edge of a table to the comfort of a deck chair. "Let's have it Peter before we go in to dress."

Peter, who had just returned from a shooting trip in India, and had been more than usually silent of late, glanced round enquiringly. We were unanimous in assent. Peter's stories, few and far between, were invariably good. As he is a far better story-teller than I shall ever be, I will give it in his own words.

"It was three months before I left for home," he commenced, "and whole yarn sounds so utterly incredible, that I'll pardon you all if you think I was mad or suffering from D.T.'s at the time. Sometimes I begin to think so myself."

For three months I had been wandering all over India slaughtering away to my heart's content, and had been more than usually successful. It was in Madras on my way down to Colombo and Home, that I met a man by name of Frobisher. We were in the bar of the Madras Club at the time, and hearing that I had been out big game shooting, he asked me if I had visited the West Coast in the course of my travels. As a matter of fact, it was about the only part that I hadn't visited, and told him so.

"Why Heaven's man," he said, "you've missed the best part of India for game. You can get elephant, tiger, bison, bear, panther, crocodile—any blinking thing you like down there."

It was off the beaten track for me, but his enthusiasm fired me. After all, I thought, I might as well do the thing properly while I was about it.

"I have a great friend down there," he continued, the light of the chase in his eye. "I'll give you an introduction to him if you like, though I haven't seen him for years now. He is as keen a sportsman as you and I'm sure would show you all the best places."

I hesitated and was lost.

"Thanks very much," I replied. "I think I'll try it. Can you tell me where your friend lives?"

"He's at a place called Munaloor, about sixty miles inland and all on his own. He plays at growing rubber, but has ample private means, and spends a large portion of his time out shooting. He's a bachelor and middle aged, but I warn you he's a bit of a crank in many ways. I expect you'll hit it off all right though."

The following day there came a note round to my hotel from Frobisher, containing the letter of introduction and a brief note wishing me luck and deploring his inability to come with me. As a post-script was another warning about his friend's eccentricies. God! if I'd only known then what those eccentricies were!

I won't bore you with my journey across the Coast. I went over by car, taking it easily and thoroughly enjoying the four hundred mile trip. At the small Club on the coast where I stayed the night before starting off inland, I made enquiries about my perspective host, whose name, I had learnt, was Anderson. Information was very vague—an unusual thing in a part where Europeans are few and far between. Anderson was not a member of the Club, and very rarely, it appeared, ever visited the town. I gathered he was a bit of a hermit, who spent his entire time on the Estate and was rarely seen by anyone. He was twenty miles from his nearest neighbours, and discouraged any attempt at social intercourse. My informants were rather tickled at the idea of my paying him a visit, but wished me luck.

All this didn't sound too encouraging, but the next day I set out hoping for the best. The first thirty miles of road proved excellent, but after leaving the main road, which carried straight on to the Nilgiris towering above me, and taking a branch road, the surface got steadily worse and worse. For the first few miles there were paddy fields and cocoanut groves, but as I went further, these gradually disappeared until eventually I was driving over what was little more than a footpath, with dense jungle on either side. Twice I skirted fairly large rubber estates, but after leaving them I saw no sign of cultivation or human residence at all with the exception of a few odd clusters of wretched grass huts, occupied by a local jungle tribe.

I had not left the coast until fairly late, and on account of the condition of the road, it was dusk by the time I reached Munaloor Estate. To my surprise it was beautifully kept and evidently run on scientific and up-to-date lines. The coolies quarters were filled with contented looking natives, who regarded me and my car with evident surprise. Everywhere were signs of prosperity. The misgivings which I had felt before began to melt. The man who ran a show like this couldn't be the bear that rumour described.

A turn in the road and a steepish climb brought me to his Bungalow, and as I twisted my way up the drive, amidst masses of tropical flowers. I experienced an odd feeling of elation and apprehension at its appearance. That doesn't sound possible, but it's the only way I can describe it.

The Bungalow itself was a big one, but of the most bizarre and fantastic construction imaginable. Eastern and Western architecture seemed to have blended, and the result, though undoubtedly attractive, was so unusual as to give one a curious sense of discomfort. It was a two-storeyed building; long, rambling and highly decorated. Minarets and domes formed the roof, and were painted gold. A large low verandah composed the front, but was rendered gloomy by numerous large and over-decorated pillars. The whole building was painted cream instead of the usual white, and, coupled with the golden minarets, proved, as I have said before, a trifle overwhelming. I hadn't time to take in more details however, before I pulled up in front of the verandah and met my host.

Here I received another shock. I don't know quite what I had expected him to be like, but I certainly wasn't prepared for what I saw.

He was a giant of a man in every sense of the word. Six foot three at least, and almost too broad for his height. A shaggy mass of black hair covered his enormous head, while a vast black beard concealed half his face. But it was his eyes that really fascinated me. Glaring at me from under bushy black eyebrows they made me feel rather like a rabbit fascinated by a snake. There was a compelling power in them that was almost frightening, and they weren't looking any too sociable then.

It was he who broke a rather awkward pause.

"Who are you, and what do you want? I don't like visitors here."

His voice was as large and deep as his frame would indicate, and the opening wasn't exactly promising. I removed my fascinated stare and delved in my pocket.

"I have a letter of introduction here from Frobisher, whom I understand is a friend of yours. I am on a shooting trip, and wondered if you could be so kind as to put me on to some good spots."

At the mention of his friend, the giant's whole manner changed at once. His beard, which had literally seemed to bristle before, relaxed, and a singularly pleasant smile creased round his eyes, which were about all that were visible of his face.

"Friend of Frobisher's, are you? I'm afraid I must have seemed rather rude but I'm shy of strangers. Come along in and have some tea; my Boys will bring in the luggage and see to the car."

He took the letter and led the way inside. Here yet another surprise awaited me. I should have been prepared for it, but somehow I wasn't. Eastern voluptiousness and Western comfort were the dominating features. Thick Persian rugs covered the floors; low divans took the place of the customary "long chairs," and were buried under masses of multi-coloured cushions; rich and highly coloured hangings and tapestries, obviously collected from all portions of the East, covered the few spaces on the walls that were not occupied by sporting trophies, and draped the numerous doors. Even the lighting—and he had electric light out there in the jungle,—was unusual. Cunningly concealed, and softly coloured bulbs, threw a diffused light over the place, and I could have sworn that there was a kind of incense burning somewhere. The centre room, into which he brought me, extended the whole height of the building, and had as ceiling one of the golden domes,—painted gold inside also,—and a balcony formed by the second storey which ran all round it. I felt rather as if I had stepped straight into a Drury Lane production of the "Arabian Nights," and half expected to see scantily clad dancing girls enter. And the extraordinary part was that he seemed to fit into the picture in spite of his European clothes.

He must have seen my look of astonishment, for he smiled again.

"I'm afraid you must think this a bit out of the ordinary"—I rather liked that. 'A bit out of the ordinary,'—I should damn well think so, "but think you will find it fairly comfortable."

I have to confess that it was. After tea, a grave and bearded servant,—no South Indian he, but a Pathan from the North,—led me to my room, where I found my dinner jacket, which by luck I had brought, laid out, and a hot bath in a sunken marble bathroom awaiting.

Dinner that night I rather dreaded. I had visions of us reclining on divans and eating our food off golden platters, but I found that I had no need for alarm, as my host was apparently perfectly normal in that respect, and after a preliminary cocktail, we sat down at a gleaming ebony table with glittering glassware and spotless linen.

Anderson, looking really magnificent in his dinner jacket, with which he wore a scarlet "cumberbund," chatted agreeably of his views on life.

"I don't like visitors," he said, "partly because they would not understand all this," with a gesture towards the ornate surroundings, "but chiefly because I find the average human being is almost entirely devoid of brains,—and I can't stand idiots. I have planned out my own method of living, and have my own particular hobbies and vices. Ordinary people might object to them. For instance, I keep what is termed a harem, and dabble in what would probably be called 'black art.' Well-meaning busy bodies would doubtless attempt to reform me if they knew about it, so for the sake of peace I shut myself off from the outside world."

I felt singularly small. I have no pretence to intellect, and whatever may be my public opinion on "harems" and "black art," I don't somehow agree with them in practice. But this black bearded giant completely overwhelmed me with his personality. One of his hobbies was a study of the natives of South India, and his stories of their different habits and customs kept me enthralled throughout dinner and the coffee and liqueurs which followed. Only once again did he refer to "black art."

"The jungle tribe of this part," he said, "are one of the most primitive races in the world and yet have control over powers of which the rest of the world knows nothing."

I was interested and asked for details, but he shut up at once.

"No, no, not now. We must be up early to-morrow if we are to do any shooting, and I don't want you to go having nightmares. I have a little wooden shack about fifteen miles from here which I use for trips of this kind and make my headquarters. It is quite near a settlement of the jungle tribe I was referring to, and I find them very useful as 'shikaris' and general porters. If you have any breeches and putties. I advise you to wear them to-morrow as the jungle is teeming with leeches at this time of year. In the meantime we had better be getting to be if we are to be up at four-thirty in the morning."

Peter paused awhile here and took a sip of the whisky and soda by his side, while the rest of us settled ourselves more comfortably in our chairs in anticipation of the second half of his story.

"I am sorry to have taken so long over the preliminaries," he resumed, "but it is essential that you should try and grasp the character of this man to follow what happened during that shooting trip."

It was gloriously fine when we set out early next morning after a small breakfast. The rains had just finished and Nature was at her best and brightest. The sun, which rose shortly after we left the Bungalow, seemed to shine on a cleansed and refreshed world and even as it dispelled the morning mists, had not as yet enough power to cause any discomfort. My host, as he strode along beside me, informed me that he kept this shack prepared all the year round, so that we could stay out as long as we wished.

"There are ibex on those hills," he continued, pointing to the towering outskirts of the Nilgiris, on whose sides the pearl grey mists were slowly dissolving, "but they are wily creatures, and we will be lucky if we get one."

He chatted away cheerily of the various adventures he had had out shooting and it was evident that he was a great "shikari." Soon after this we left the friendly rubber trees and the narrowness of

the jungle path and the density of the under growth, put an end
to further conversation.

The West Coast jungle is different to that of the rest of India.
An extremely heavy rainfall, and a damp, sticky heat, make for
luxuriant growth and as we pushed our way along, with giant trees
and exotic creepers and flowers around us, I felt strangely awed
by the magnificence of it all. My companion was evidently more
wideawake, for as I dreamed, there came the sharp crash of his
gun, and a jungle fowl, which had rashly chosen that moment to
fly across the path, fell almost at my feet.

"Something for the pot," he smiled, handing it over to one of
the coolies who was carrying our kit.

As I have said, it was only fifteen miles, but fifteen miles through
the jungle takes some doing, and I was glad enough when we came
into the little clearing which contained the natives' grass huts and
was told that the shack was only a few hundred yards ahead.

Anderson stopped awhile and chatted with the natives, who
to me resembled apes more than men, and I noticed a curious look
in their eyes, which later I realized was a mixture of awe and fright.
He was apparently something of God to them, and although he
seemed to speak kindly enough, I could detect the ring of authority
in his voice and read abject submission in their eyes and manner.

The hut proved to be, as he said, only a bamboo and thatch
affair, but was furnished inside in the same weird manner as his
Bungalow. He evidently believed in doing his shooting in comfort,—
in fact he admitted so to me, but somehow I couldn't help wishing,
even that first night, that the place wasn't quite so comfortable.

It all seemed so unreal: so fantastic, and there was a definite feeling of repulsion about this lonely hut in the depths of the jungle—a feeling akin to that which had struck me when I first saw his Bungalow,—only more pronounced.

For a complete week, however, it seemed as if my apprehensions were unfounded. We had excellent sport in every way, and I was lucky enough to bag two fine bison bulls and an ibex. Anderson was the perfect host and kept me amused night after night with his strange philosophy and endless stock of yarns.

It was on the evening before we started back for home that things happened, and I feel quite creepy even now at the thought of them.

We had had a fairly strenuous day and had returned just before nightfall, with a sambhur stag and a huge boar "tusker" by way of trophies. After an excellent dinner we were lazing amongst the cushions of his divans chatting desultorily. I remember that it was I who brought the subject up first. We happened to be talking on religion, and remembering Anderson's references to "black art," I asked him casually if he thought there was anything in the doings of some of the famous Spiritualists.

He eyed me as if weighing me up, and evidently finding the inspection satisfactory, burst forth:

" 'Anything in it.' Of course there's something in it—there's everything in it, but those idiots at home are merely blundering around the edges of the subject. They think, when they make tables knock, and shapes materialize, that they are invoking spirits,—the poor brainless fools. They are toying with the greatest power on earth, and know nothing of it. They don't realize their danger, and never will until someone accidently stumbles on the truth,— and then he probably won't live to tell it."

I was keenly interested and even rather excited.

"I'm afraid I can't quite follow what you are talking about. What is this 'power' to which you refer?"

The light of fanaticism was burning in the man's eye, but his reply was sober enough.

"It is something that took me years to discover, and even then I only found it in the end by accident. I think I have mentioned before that these Tiamurs,"—referring to the jungle tribe near whose settlement we were living—"have powers that no one else on earth possesses. From them I accidently learnt the secret, but given the necessary clue, have raised that power to be something more than it will ever be to them and have gone many stages further than they ever will. You won't understand the full psychological details, so I am going to put it as simply as I can. You may have read in the papers of an experiment conducted which proved that the human eye has a slight power of attraction. In this case I believe, it was demonstrated that the 'rays', or whatever you like to call them, issuing from a man's eye, were powerful enough to move a small object suspended from a hair, and cause it to oscillate slightly. I, at that time, was dabbling in so-called Spiritualism and I recall finding, after reading that article— which seemed to draw no great public attention—that it fitted in with a theory which I had already begun to form. Then suddenly out here, I hit on the truth. I won't trouble you with how it happened, but will tell you of the stage which I have now reached. It's a difficult thing to explain, but I'll do my best."

I shifted to a more comfortable position amongst the cushions and waited for this remarkable man to continue.

"The human brain is a marvellous affair—far more wonderful than even the leading psychologists dream. They do not know, for example that from the moment of birth until death, the cells of our brains are ceaselessly sending out what, for lack of a better word, I will call 'rays'. Neither do they know that these 'rays' have the most extraordinary powers. They succeeded in proving that the eye could move matter, but there they dropped the subject. Little did they realize that the eye was then merely concentrating those brain 'rays' and that given time and practice, the brain is capable of moving far more than a mere scrap of metal dangling from a hair."

He must have seen the doubt in my eyes, for he pointed to an ordinary walking stick leaning against the wall at the other side of the room.

"Watch," he said curtly.

I looked; rubbed my eyes and looked again. It was true and I wasn't dreaming. *The walking stick was moving slowly across the room,—upright and of its own accord!*

I was too spellbound even to be frightened, and turned my gaze to his face. His eyes were fixed on the stick and the pupils had narrowed down to mere pin-points. Almost could I imagine those "rays" of his issuing from his brilliant eyes.

He took the stick as it reached him and threw it over to me. I examined it with care. It was solid enough in all conscience.

He regarded me with shining eyes.

"Frightened?"

I shook my head dumbly. I was—but I wasn't going to admit it.

"No," he said, continuing his talk as if there had been no interruption, "there is nothing to be frightened of in that, but it's when we reach the next stage that in the hands of amateurs, the danger arises. Shall I go on?"

I nodded, still incapable of speech.

"Even the Tiamurs can do *that*, and so can our scientific and spiritualistic friends at home,—on a minor scale. They can even go a step further and use those rays to *make* matter—but they don't realize it. When they see a ghostly face in a darkened room, or feel beastly animals crawling or flapping their wings, they think they have invoked some long dead spirit. What they really see, however, is the creation of their own minds, or rather of their sub-conscious minds. Science has long ago proved that the entire universe, including you and me, is composed of atoms. Constantly they are trying to smash atoms, or some such foolishness, little knowing that from the human brain alone the necessary power can be generated. 'Rays' that are sufficient to attract the atoms which compose an object, are also invested with further powers,—those of disintegrating and re-assembling atoms in any form that the brain may desire. The 'ghosts' that spiritualists see are the result of their inadvertent use of this power, and therein lies their danger. I have the advantage that I know what I am playing with—they don't."

He paused a while and I began to wonder whether it was all a ghastly nightmare or not. Before I had time to speak, he had commenced again.

"So far have I got, my friend, but here temporarily I have to admit defeat. I can create something out of nothing. I can make a stone where there was no stone before, *but* those creations remain a part of me, and one the relaxation of my will power they depart into the void out of which they came. If I could separate them from myself. I would achieve the ambition of my life, and control a power sufficient to rule the world." And he finished triumphantly. "*I am on the verge of obtaining that power.*"

I stared at him fascinated: horror incredulity and terror on my face. He looked at me in amusement.

"You evidently don't believe me. I will have to give you another demonstration."

I shook my head beseechingly, but he was too engrossed with his subject.

"Think of some definite object, will you," he demanded. "Not too large for convenience's sake. The brain, like a wireless set, has its receiving as well as its transmitting apparatus. If you think hard enough of anything, my brain will receive your thoughts and reproduce the object of them for you. All I ask of you is to remain where you are and not touch either me or it."

My curiosity overcame my terror, but for the life of me I could find nothing suitable to think of. Finally in despair, I started thinking of one of the beautiful champagne glasses that we had used in his Bungalow that first night. It was a lovely thing of purest glass with a long tapering stem and delicately tinted lip, and the memory of it was still strong in my mind. I glanced at Anderson as I thought. He was half sitting, half lying on a divan some eight feet away, and separated from me only by a low lacquer table. His eyes, as on the previous occasion, were wide open, but with the pupils contracted to mere pin points while their gaze was concentrated on the table between us. I shrank back in mortal terror from what I felt was going to happen, but my eyes were fascinated—fixed. It happened! Before my very eyes it happened! In the subdued light of that little room, the fruit of my brain was born out of the very air, and as if prove its reality, Anderson stretched out a huge arm and rapped its edges until it rang. It was too much for my frayed nerves. I put my arms before my face as if to ward off a blow and to shut out the sight of that slender glittering "thing".

"Stop, stop," I almost shrieked. "It's—it's blasphemy."

The next thing I can remember distinctly was the fizz of on opening soda water bottle, and looking up from the shelter of my arms, found Anderson standing beside me pouring soda into a good stiff peg of whisky.

"Here drink this my son," he said quite gently. "I was a damned fool to go showing off my parlour tricks. They are things I have never shown anybody,—except the Tiamurs, and even they don't like them."

I grabbed at the whisky gladly enough and Anderson became his usual courteous self, but I was thankful when dawn broke next morning, and after a sleepless night I was able to get away from the scene of those nightmare experiments into what seemed the clear, uncontaminated air of the jungle.

Anderson enquired solicitously after my health, and again expressed regret at having scared me so.

"I'm afraid that I was carried away by my enthusiasm," he said. "I will be grateful if you will keep all that you have seen and heard to yourself,—at any rate unless you hear from me."

I promised him readily enough. I didn't want to be considered more of a liar than I was already.

The morning was clear and fine, but even in the pleasant twilight of the jungle I was still feeling nervous, and hurried on determined to set off for civilization in the car that day rather than spend another night with Anderson. In order to travel quicker, we had left our guns with the luggage coolies and after some three hours brisk tramping, were some way on ahead of them.

As we were crossing a small track of swampy ground. Anderson leant forward and examined some marks in the mud.

"I see that our old friend the 'rogue' elephant has just come along here," he remarked. "He can't be very far ahead either, as the water is only just beginning to filter into his tracks."

"How do you know he is a 'rogue,'" I asked, "Is this another exhibition of your supernatural powers?"

Anderson laughed good naturedly.

"No. I happen to know that he is the 'rogue' from the fact that one of his feet is slightly deformed and smaller than the others. He has been hanging around the countryside for some time, and besides doing a lot of damage to the Estate, is reputed to have killed several coolies. I hope we don't meet him with only walking sticks in our hands. I've half a mind to wait for our rifles."

I succeeded in persuading him to come on, but a few minutes later bitterly regretted my impetuosity.

We had passed into one of those occasional small clearings in the jungle where thick grass was growing shoulder high. We had got nearly three-quarters of the way across it when suddenly from the other side, came the shrill, unmistakable 'trumpet' of an angry elephant, and the next instant the jungle parted and the enormous bulk of a solitary tusker came charging down towards us.

A charging elephant is an unpleasant sight even under the most favourable circumstances but when one is standing defenceless in a clearing with the nearest tree some seventy-five yards away, the unpleasantness becomes acute.

"Run," came Anderson's voice curtly, "For your life."

I needed no bidding; I was already running, but I had only gone a few yards when I somehow sensed that my companion wasn't following. I glanced over my shoulder as I raced along, and the sight which I saw pulled me up dead in my tracks.

Alone out there in the clearing stood Anderson, waiting the charging elephant, and as I watched, I saw him raise a heavy rifle to his shoulder and aim deliberately at the only vulnerable spot of a head-on elephant,—the centre of its forehead. Came the ear splitting crash of a 450 Express and the elephant, staggering forward a few paces, fell head foremost to the ground, almost on top of the prostrate figure of Anderson, who had crumpled up on the report of the rifle. I dashed back horror-stricken, but was too late. They were both dead when I reached them."

Peter paused again and finished his drink.

"But I thought," said Yvonne, "that you had left your rifles behind."

Peter hesitated.

"We had," he said slowly at last. *"When I reached his body all that was lying at his side was his walking stick."*

There was a deathly silence as Peter's voice completed the tale.

"We carried him back to the Bungalow, and the Doctor whom I brought back next day after an all night run, declared death due to heart failure. I didn't tell him the full yarn—I didn't want to be ridiculed—so, as the natives weren't saying anything, I let him have his own way. Any rate it would have done no good. Poor Anderson had achieved his ambition and in doing so had saved my life and lost his own."

Peter fished in a pocket and pulled out a small battered lump of lead: obviously the spent bullet of a high velocity rifle. We crowded round to examine it.

"I found that next day in the dead elephant's brain," he said simply.

From *The Madras Mail Annual* (1930)

The Aryan Smiles

by J. Warton and N. Blenman

IT SHALL EVER BE ONE OF MY GREATEST REGRETS THAT I DID not go with Michael Clancey on the evening he met his untimely death. If I had not been able to prevent it, I might, at least, have consoled a pious widow and daughter with the thought that his soul still lingered for the charity of their prayers, and that his end had not been the awful one of suicide. Not that they inclined to the latter view, but they feared it, while, with the mentality of simple Irish Catholics, they naturally acquiesced in the superstitious explanation of a very bizarre incident.

Whereas I might, then, have been able to bring into the light of human reason at least one of these happenings in a community where too ready a credence is placed in the damnable Black Arts of the Orient, it is to a mind, sceptical and materialistic as mine, the more galling to have to relate only the remarkable facts concerning the loss of a very dear friend.

"Mike," I had said, "I can't go with you to-night, much as I would love to have a drive"—and much as I liked his company; for we used to spend many an evening chatting of our military days, and Mike, bluff and quick-tempered, had been the most popular man in the Battery.

We had come to India together, and like so many soldiers in the old days, we had been glad to take up quieter occupations and to remain in the country. The growing railway systems offered a good field for employment, and my friend had joined the Southern Punjab and Delhi Railway; on this comparatively small section of railroad, he had had a somewhat meteoric career. As Station Master of Delhi, and a man not yet forty-five, he had reason to exult in his change of professions, for he might otherwise have been plain Farrier-Sergeant Clancey.

I had been lucky to get in with a firm of piecegoods merchants. One of our more important men was up from Calcutta, and as I had a semi-business dinner to attend that evening, I did not feel quite up to the conviviality which Michael Clancey would be sure to lead me into: although there was time for a little outing before dinner, I had preferred to entertain him at my bungalow. After an half-hour's tete-a-tete and a couple of mild whiskies on the verandah, he had climbed into his dog-cart alone, cracked his whip and turned sharply out my gate. It was a sultry July evening. Before going in to dress, I stood outside for a few minutes listening to the fine even patter of his Waler's hoofs get fainter and fainter down the long quiet road. I had seen and heard the last of Mike Clancey for ever, but did not know it then.

It must have been 7-30 when he left me; an hour later I was at the hotel at which I was to dine. Four of us sat down to dinner.

We were well into our cigars when I received the following note. On top of the small envelope was written "Urgent, Please deliver at once." Excusing myself, I read:—

"Dear Mr. Warton,—Mr. Clancey's syce, who is the bearer of this, will tell you more than I can. Being a friend of Mr. Clancey's, I am sure you will question the man at once. I am nervous about it myself, and shall tell you the reasons for my anxiety if you would call over now.—Yours sincerely,—Marie Smythe."

Mrs. Smythe was one of the Railway colony. I think her husband was the Plate-Layer. My friend was boarding with the Smythes at the time while his wife and daughter were in the Hills.

Somewhat disconcerted at receiving this vague note, I crumpled it into my pocket, and, leaving the company as nicely as I could, went downstairs to hear what the groom had to say. He had come down in his master's dog-cart; the horse was champing and sneezing over his head while he gave me a story, which, coupled with Mrs. Smythe's note, was sufficiently alarming, although the whole affair bore a very queer aspect indeed.

For a time I wondered whether it warranted my leaving the dinner party. I told the syce to wait, however, and went back to my fellow-diners for a few minutes and even had another drink. Being uneasy all the time, and as it was nearly ten o'clock, I decided at last to go. Saying boldly that a friend had been suddenly taken ill, and receiving from each one a laconic "I'm sorry!" as he rose to shake hands, I bid my companions "Good-night."

Sitting by the syce, while he drove me to Mrs. Smythe's, I got him to recount his brief story.

"The Sahib went out first at seven o'clock," he said.

"Yes, yes," I put in, "he came to see me."

"Well, he returned home, called for the whisky, sat a while on the 'chabutra', and then we drove off towards the Roshanara Gardens. Sahib often went there before dinner 'to take the air'. He would walk round the Gardens, leaving me to hold the horse. This evening, I thought it rather late for the master's usual drive. However, it was still lightsome when he pulled up in the Gardens. He alighted and went off in the direction of the Tank. Holding the reins, I sat down on the gravel walk. But the Sahib being longer than I thought he would, I eventually took the horse and buggy a few paces off on to the lawn, where I secured the reins to a small tree, gave the animal his fodder from the cart, and began to smoke myself.

"In this way, Sahib, I had consumed two or three 'biris', strolling about some times to see if the master was in sight; and the horse meanwhile had finished his bag of hay.

"There was no sign of the Sahib, and we must have been out more than an hour—he usually dined by half-past-eight—so I walked all round the Gardens. After waiting another short while, I drove back to the 'kothi' without him, then inquired at Smythe Memsahib's, who sent me back to the Gardens at once to look for my master; but I did not stay there more than a few minutes. To tell you the truth, Sahib, we poor country folk are very frightened. And what was the use of waiting? So I went again to the Memsahib, after having called first at your house; and then she gave me the letter to you."

To such a narrative I had no comments to make, and waited rather curiously for Mrs. Smythe's account, which she gave me in the presence of her husband.

"We stayed dinner very long for Mr. Clancey," she said, after apologising for having called me away. This, she said, she would not have done but for the fact that Mr. Clancey had been rather unwell during the day.

"Oh," I remarked, "I didn't know that. He seemed all right when I saw him this evening."

"It's a funny thing, Mr. Warton," she went on. "A kind of fits, perhaps; though I have never seen anything like it before. At breakfast Mr. Clancey complained of feeling very hot. He said his skin was burning. I suggested 'prickly heat'; but he assured me it wasn't that, and began to eat quite heartily. Suddenly we saw his face go as red as a turkey-cock's; he jumped from the table, tearing off his collar and unbuttoning his coat. 'Fiends alive, Fiends alive, Mrs. Smythe!' he shouted, grabbing at his clothes. 'I'll go home!' 'No, go into the bedroom, Mr. Clancey,' I said. 'What's the matter?' throwing off his coat, he went inside, supported by my husband."

"With his shirt off", added Mr. Smythe, "he ran straight to the bathroom, and ducked his head in the tub. 'I'm on fire, Smythe,' he cried. 'Splash it on hard!' and we drenched him to the waist with mugfuls of cold water, you could see the very blood glowing under his skin, but it soon got back its natural whiteness, and he sat down with us and finished his meal."

Mrs. Smythe continued the account.

"We saw him again at tea time," she told me. "He had just come from his round at the Station, as usual. He ate very little, but drank an enormous quantity of tea, saying there was nothing like tea for cooling the system. It has been a very hot day, as you know, and we did not think too much of Mr. Clancey's discomfort. However, I took his temperature before he went home; he had no fever."

"In that case," I said, rising impatiently, "it might be that poor Clancey is lying in an apoplectic fit, or something of the kind— I wonder whether this man looked properly!—I had better go to the Gardens and see."

Smythe offered to accompany me, and we set off to the Roshanara Gardens. On the way I had more details of my friend's misfortune.

"My wife had not time to tell you," began Smythe; "but what has been troubling her most is damn queer—the sort of thing you might have no patience with; I have little time myself for these tales—But I may as well tell it to you. Now, these queer symptoms of Clancey's, when he complained of his flesh being on fire—these may be anything at all. But he told us blandly that he thought it was the jogi's curse."

"The jogi's curse?" I said.

"Yes," reiterated Smythe, "the jogi's curse. And when he said this, my wife became very solemn, telling him it was not right to jest about such things. But let me explain.

"Now, you know how hot-headed Clancey is. It appears that last evening he maltreated one of these religious mendicants—he told us about it at dinner. He was driving through the Station garden when he noticed this sadhu fellow on the grass-plot. The man had set up a few bricks, lit a fire, and was preparing his evening meal. What Clancey said to him I don't know, and he probably had good reason to be annoyed, for he has practically made that garden with his own hands; but he should not have struck the fellow,—though he told us about it very sadly afterwards. As a matter of fact, he is too fond of that horsewhip of his, using it on the Station staff at times; in spite of it, they are fond of him. Anyhow, he says the jogi was insolent, that he laughed and went on with his cooking. The Station Master riled that his authority should be so flouted, dismounted from his dog-cart, whip in hand, and ordered the trespasser out of the garden; when he still would not go, Clancey lashed the smiling Hindu three or four times across the back. The jogi poured some water on to the fire, and, drawing out the moistened ashes from his 'chulah', threw it in handfuls over his naked body, applying the emolient especially to his smarting wounds. Then, holding up his skinny hands and pointing heavenward, he muttered something which Irishman took to be oaths and curses. He says the man finally gathered up his things, spat on the ground, and went away, but not without looking round at Clancey and saying: 'The Almighty has a Lash of Retribution! Its thongs are Flames of Fire!'"

"But," I protested, "Clancey wouldn't understand all that."

"I believe one of his babus overheard, and translated it for him," explained Smythe.

"An eloquent piece of nonsense!" I said. "But, of course, it's just possible Clancey has been ailing from the weather. It has been a particularly hot day."

In this part of India the Monsoon is often very feeble. Here we were at the end of July, and still panting for the rain. The sky, however, had been overcast all day, which made the heat the more unbearable.

It was pitchy dark in the Gardens; but with the aid of a couple of railway lanterns, we eventually went over the grounds very thoroughly by eleven o'clock. During this search Smythe and I walked right under a huge peepul tree that grew on the verge of the Tank. Under this tree we missed the light from the second lantern, and, calling to the syce who carried it behind us, we saw that he stood at some distance away. He said that he would not go under that tree for love or money, and begged that we would not ask him to do so. So Smythe took the lamp from him, and we passed on after examining the ground under the tree, as we did with every other dark patch and corner of the Gardens.

There was nothing for it now but to begin a long vigil on the spot where my friend had left his dog-cart, when he had commenced his walk. About midnight Smythe went home to his wife, so I was left with the syce for company. He sat cross-legged on the grass near me, while I reclined on the cushion seat which had been removed from the trap.

Feeling the urge to engage him in conversation, there was one question that came to me at once. (The more important matter of his master's encounter with the jogi we had already thrashed out; he had been with Clancey at the time and corroborated that story). In fact, the question I put to my companion now was just an idle one, for I guessed the likely answer, knowing the minds of these rustic folk regarding such things as phantoms and spooks. The tree he had been so afraid of, I thought, is probably haunted by a she-devil, the well-known 'churail'. Anyhow, "Syce", I said, "why wouldn't you come under that peepul tree with us?"

"No Hindu would, Sahib," he answered, "unless he were a stranger in Delhi."

"No? And why not?"

"How shall I tell you? You white people laugh at these things. But you must have heard it when you were under the tree."

"Heard what?"

"Didn't you hear him smoking his hookah?.... T-oo-r-r-.... T-oo-r-r-r?"

"What?" I said. "In the branches of the tree?—That was a night-bird of some kind!" And I laughed.

"For this reason," he said indignantly, "I did not wish to say anything about the cursed tree."

However certain I felt that this simple-minded Hindu had mistaken the croaking of some nocturnal creature for the bubbling and gurgling drawl of a hookah, I was ready to hear any old story, and cajoled him into telling me a rather good one.

"In the first place," I said, "why do you call it a cursed tree? The peepul is sacred to you Hindus."

"Yes," he agreed "but this particular peepul has been cursed. It came about in this way: In the time of the Emperor Aurungzeb, a certain 'pir' took up this abode under this tree, and began to persecute the poor Hindu people who used to come to the sacred tree to offer their 'poojahs' and to bathe in the Tank. He would throw away the flowers, sweets and fruits of their sacrifices, desecrate their altars, and beat the devotees off if necessary".

"The Hindus," I commented, "were very meek to allow the high-handed behaviour of this Mohamedan!"

"You know the fanatical Muslim Aurungzeb was," he said. "The poor Hindus could hope for no redress. And so things went on at this peepul tree, till, making a virtue of necessity, the Hindus of the neighbourhood abandoned their sacred tree to this wicked man. In fact, their veneration grew to loathing—it was considered to have been defiled. And when, eventually, the holy pir was buried on the spot where he had made his home, under the tree for some forty years, the curse was thought to be complete, and no Hindu would think of sacrificing under this peepul. One night, they say, a band of daring youths (Hindus) went to the pir's grave, exhumed the recently-interred body, and threw it into the Tank, where it remained. Since then, Sahib, the soul of that wretched pir haunts the old peepul. I heard him to-night, worse luck! You heard him too. And he is always there at the top of the tree at night, pulling away at his hubble-bubble."

"Humph!" I said, and thought I would like to go over to the tree and throw a few stones at the croaking bird which had given rise to the syce's funny story. I might have made the test, but that we had to take shelter presently under an open pavilion near by, for the long-promised rain had come at last, though at an awkward time. A high wind blew the sand into our faces, there were quick flashes of lurid lightning, and we had only just enough time to unyoke the Waler before we realised that we were exposed to an Indian sandstorm. I thought the horse would have kicked down the wooden posts of the pavilion, and that the zinc roof would have been blown over our heads, while we struggled to make the animal share the small shelter with us. Soon the elements became calmer, and so did the horse. But suddenly, as if from nowhere, there was a bluish-yellow flash and a crashing report. Looking in the direction of the sound, I heard a splashing.

"Sahib," whispered the syce, with his hand on my arm, "that is the peepul tree! It has been struck!"

These sandstorms are fiercer than they are lasting, so in a few minutes we were able to go out and examine the tree, the syce keeping at a very safe distance. Almost half of it had seen torn down and lay immersed in the water of the Tank. The other part stood gaunt and lifeless on a charred and blackened trunk. This was easily discernible, for the bark of the peepul is of a glistening light grey colour.

I had had enough of strange stories, and now had come an uncanny experience. How this fitted into a chain of apparently occult influences was shown the next morning. After an anxious night of waiting and watching, informing the police, and having no rest, we began dredging operations at the Tank; the clue for the search was Clancey's horsewhip.

Like a lost fishing-rod, it was seen to be sticking up out of the weeds close to the fallen tree. The syce recognised it at once;

he said the Sahib always took the whip with him in these little walks.

About mid-way the body of my poor friend was brought out, with all the ordinary signs of drowning apparent. The water was certainly weedy; yet Clancey could swim well. But how and why he got into the water shall never be known. And just before his body was found, one of the men brought up a vessel covered over and filled with a loamy black soil form the bottom of the Tank; when the mud was removed, the object revealed itself to be an old copper hookah.

"Throw it back!" cried the syce. "It belonged to the wicked pir!"

Whether he was right or not will also never be known.

From the *Indian State Railway Magazine* (June 1933)

Panther People

by C.A. Kincaid

ALEC BRIGGS, A TALL POWERFULLY BUILT MAN IN THE middle thirties, was driving through the Dharwar forest one cold weather morning in an ancient but still quite efficient touring car. He was superintendent of forests in the Kanara District and was on his way to confer with other forest officers, English and Indian, in Dharwar. He had come up the Ghats[1] and had a bare twenty miles to go before he reached the open plain. He knew the road well; only a few weeks before he and an English friend had driven along it and at a bend had suddenly come face to face with a tiger. The tiger had stepped with a low growl to one side; Briggs

---

1. The mountains on the western boundary of the great central plateau of India.

pressed the accelerator and the car shot past. A mile or so farther on they had met two or three forest women picking up sticks for fuel. Greatly excited, they had shouted to them to get into the car and escape; a tiger was close by. The women had declined the invitation with a smile. "The old tiger," they said, "why, we see him every day. He is quite harmless; he never hurts anyone." Indeed in their indulgent contempt they even neglected to call him 'they'—the royal privilege to which all tigers are entitled. Briggs smiled at the recollection and looked at the trees which surrounded him on all sides and, but for the road to guide him, would have soon engulfed him in their midst.

Just then out of a small clearing in front stepped an Englishman. He had no topi and he was dressed in a suit of a curious grey material, old but well cut and serviceable. Briggs wondered what on earth the man was doing in this wild haunted forest. He threw the gear lever into neutral, pressed his brake and pulled up close to the newcomer. As he came nearer, Briggs noticed his curious build. He must have stood six feet two, but his legs and his arms were quite short; indeed, out of all proportion to his great height. On the other hand, his body was beautifully formed with a strange catlike grace that quite made up for the shortness of his limbs.

Briggs addressed him courteously and said: "Hullo! What's the matter? Can I help you at all? I expect you have lost your way."

The stranger answered in a pleasant well-bred voice: "No, I have not got lost. I know this forest well; besides I have a useful bump of locality. I am on a shooting expedition. I was just walking to my camp. Still, as it is some way off near the edge of the forest, I should be glad of a lift."

"Right-o!" said Briggs, cordially. "Come along inside. I'll tell you what. We'll drive to a glade I know of a couple of miles ahead and there we'll have breakfast. I have a tiffin basket at the back and I shall be very glad indeed if you'll join me."

"It is most awfully kind of you. My name is Savile. I used to be in the 82nd, but I retired three years ago and now I am just loafing about and shooting when I get the chance."

The car did not take long to carry the forest officer and his guest to the glade of which the former had spoken. Briggs opened the door and got out; he lifted the tiffin basket from the back to a convenient mound. The basket was amply furnished, for its owner liked to do himself well when on the march. Two large flasks held hot tea. Polished white dishes, cups, saucers, plates and cutlery of all kinds offered every aid to the consumption of cold chicken and tongue, ham, pressed beef, currant cake and fruit that awaited the hunger of the travellers.

Briggs carved the chicken and gave his newly-found friend an ample portion. Savile snatched the plate so greedily that Briggs thought to himself 'the poor devil must be starving.' Certainly Savile polished off his helping in no time and was quite ready for a second before Briggs, stout trencherman though he was, had really started on his first. Then Savile said in his clear well-bred voice: "Are you not afraid to go through this forest alone?"

"No," said Briggs with some surprise, "why?"

"Well, of course, it may only be idle gossip; but I have heard from some trustworthy natives that there are panther people about."

Briggs began to wonder whether his guest was not an escaped lunatic; so, instead of asking him incredulously what the devil he meant, he said as calmly as he could: "No, I have never heard that; but what are panther people exactly?"

"They are men and women who have the power to turn themselves into panthers at will; or perhaps they may be panthers that have the power to turn themselves into men and women. After all it does not matter much, for it comes to the same in the end, doesn't it?" And Savile smiled whimsically.

Briggs began to grow deeply interested: "You surely have never met such people, have you?"

"Well, yes. I was so unfortunate some four years ago as to marry one of them."

This was more than Briggs could stand: "I wish the deuce, old chap, you wouldn't try to pull my leg. You cannot expect me to believe such a yarn as that."

Savile's courteous manner never changed. "Well, such a statement does seem rather tall in cold blood; but if you like I'll tell you my story and then you can believe it or not, as you please...."

"Yes, do."

"Some eight years ago I had just got my majority and I thought it was time to marry. Subalterns, you know, are expected to remain bachelors. Married captains are not always popular; but majors are more or less required to have wives. So I began to look for a suitable lady."

"When a man begins to look for a wife, it is wonderful how soon he finds a lady who seems to be his long-looked-for ideal. I met my soul's mate at Dhulia in Khandesh, where her father held a post on the railway. After her marriage she insisted on spending our honeymoon shooting the great jungles of Western Khandesh; and she never seemed so happy as when we were camping in the forest. After our honeymoon we went to Mhow, where my regiment was stationed and the rainy season passed very pleasantly with polo, cricket and tennis—the usual military life, you know. My wife was a bit of a flirt; but I did not mind that. She had only just come out when I married her and I realised that she was wild to enjoy to the full the new life she had just begun to know."

"Among her favourite squires was a Civil Servant, a man called Trevelyan, who was in the Political Department and was officiating as first assistant to Sir William Thompson, the Agent to the Governor-General in Central India. Trevelyan was a good-looking, well-set-up man and I liked him personally so much that I never dreamt of being jealous of his friendly relations with my wife. When in November we received and invitation to spend ten days at Christmas in the Agent's camp at Bundelkhand, I guessed, and rightly, that Trevelyan had got us the invitation. My wife was delighted at the idea of camping in Central India. I was overjoyed at the thought of bagging my first tiger."

"Well, to make a long story short, we reached our destination on Christmas Eve. Although there were not many guests there was an abundance of large and luxurious tents, while a huge *shamiana*,[2] divided into two parts, served as a dining room and a drawing room. The Agent to the Governor-General had invited eight guns and three of them, including myself, had brought their wives. A big drive was fixed for Christmas Day and H.H. the Maharaja of

---

2. Large state tent.

Ortha, who owned the jungle where we were camping, had done some splendid staff work. He did not take part in the shoot; but I saw him one day when he came to call on the Agent."

"Did you know him?" asked Savile, pausing.

"No," said Briggs, "I am afraid my acquaintance with Maharajas is somewhat limited."

"Well, if you had seen him once you would never forget him. He stood six feet high and was very handsome; his bearing was such as can only be found in a Rajput chief who claims descent through two hundred generations from the divine Ramachandra himself. However, I must not begin telling you about Hindu divinities and Rajput descents or I shall never finish. I must get on with my story.

"My wife and I had separate tents—it was her wish always to sleep alone as she said I snored so badly that I disturbed her— and our tents stood at the edge of the encampment. On Christmas Day we all met cheerfully in the big tent for tea and eggs and toast and to wish each other a Merry Christmas; then we set out. Most of the way we were carried on the Maharaja's elephants—interesting at first but slow after a bit, for their maximum speed is some two miles an hour. When we got near the place where the tigers were supposed to be lying up, we got off the kneeling elephants and walked to the *machans* assigned to us. I was rather a junior, so I was given an outside place and never really expected to shoot anything: nevertheless, in big game shooting luck lies upon the knees of the gods.

"Suddenly I heard the heavy, dull footfalls of a great beast and into the open space below my tree stepped a magnificent male tiger. It was in the prime of life, brilliantly striped and wearing its deep winter fur. I took careful aim at the point of its shoulder and fired. It fell; I gave it a second barrel and then, reloading, waited, hoping for another animal. Then I heard two shots with a little interval between them; they came from the direction of the A.G.G.'s *machan* and I guessed that he had secured a tiger too. I was right. When the beaters came up, we compared our experiences. There had been a tiger and a tigress in the beat. I had got the one and my host the other."

"You were jolly lucky," murmured Briggs, "to bag a tiger in your first beat."

"Yes; I was, and there was no lighter-hearted guest in the A.G.G.'s camp that evening at dinner; but now I am coming to the sinister side of the story. I am afraid I am boring you?" Savile paused on a note of interrogation.

"No, please do go on: I am deeply interested."

"Very well. Next morning as we sat in the big tent at our tea and toast, a young fellow, Howard of the Central India Horse, rushed in greatly excited. Addressing Sir William Thompson, he cried: 'I say, Sir, a panther came into our camp last night. There are pugs³ close to my tent and just outside Trevelyan's!' His statement brought answering cries of 'Rot!' 'Not really!' and we all ran out to see the panther's tracks. Yes; there they were. There was no doubt about it. The beast could not have been very large, six foot six or seven foot at most judging from its footprints.

---

3. Tracks.

"After talking the subject threadbare, we turned to other topics. That day we beat another part of the jungle but drew a blank. Next morning Howard again brought news of fresh panther's tracks in the camp. This time they were visible outside my wife's tent. I began to get seriously alarmed. Trevelyan, too, looked so shocked at the news that I thought he was going to faint. Whether Sir William noticed his assistant's weakness or not, I do not know; but, if he did, he covered it by saying: 'I tell you what. One of you fellows must sit up for the panther this evening close to the camp. We'll tie up a goat and it will probably come about five or so this afternoon. It must be desperately hungry and quite unafraid of men, or it would not enter my camp at night. Will you sit up for it, Savile?'

"I agreed readily, and after tea, on our return from another drive in which Jowers, the Superintendent of Police, bagged a bear, I went and sat up in a tree a couple of hundred yards from the camp. A goat was brought and tied up, but there was not sign of a panther. No monkeys chattered; no birds struck warning notes; even the goat seemed perfectly calm and collected. It grazed for a while and then lay down quietly; so far as I could judge, it fell fast asleep.

"I was disgusted, as you can imagine. At the same time I could not get out of my head Trevelyan's appearance at *chota hazri*. I had begun indeed to regret having accepted Sir William's invitation. The first and second evenings Trevelyan had been too attentive to my wife for my liking, but the third day he had seemed to avoid her and all the fourth day he had appeared to be terrified of her.

"Just before dinner time I slipped out of my tree, went to my tent and changed for dinner."

"I am generally a very sound sleeper; but whether I had eaten or drunk too much, I found myself wide awake at two o'clock in the morning. I was about to turn over when I saw in the bright moonlight—it was nearly full moon—a panther pass close by the *chicks* (screen) of my tent. It was warm and I had not let down the *kanats*.[4] I did not know quite what to do. I was frankly afraid. I thought the best thing was to wait a minute or two and then peep out. I did so, and putting my head through the tent door, I looked about for the panther. It had vanished! Then I went to my wife's tent. It was empty! Her nightdress lay on her bed and her slippers under it. For a moment I thought that she might have paid Trevelyan's tent a visit and the blood rushed to my head; but I grew calm again as I saw that all her clothes lay on her chair. I decided not to make myself ridiculous by rushing into Trevelyan's tent. I would get back to bed and wait until my wife returned and ask her. Once, however, under the bedclothes, I fell asleep and did not wake until my wife came into my tent fully dressed to ask me whether I was not going to have any *chota hazri*. I pulled on my clothes as quickly as I could and went to the dining room.

"There I found more excitement. Fresh tracks had been noticed outside my tent this time and again outside Trevelyan's. I looked at Trevelyan. His appearance was ghastly; rising from his place, he excused himself, pleading fever. I asked my wife later why she

---

4. Canvas door of tent.

had left her tent in the night: she looked me in the face and, laughing, asked me what I meant. When I told her that I had entered her tent and found her bed empty and her nightdress lying on her bed, she said: 'My dear boy, you must have been dreaming. Is it likely that I should walk about the camp at 2 a.m. stark naked?' I could find no answer and for a time I really thought that I must have been dreaming. I resolved, nevertheless, to keep awake the following night, rifle in hand, and shoot the panther should it come again into camp. I told no one, not even my wife, of my intention. I was afraid that everyone else would want to sit up, too, and the panther would be scared.

"After dinner I drew my chair close behind the *chick* of my tent and, as before, I did not lower the *kanat*. I kept awake until one, and then I must have dropped off to sleep. About two I awoke with a start and saw in the brilliant moonlight the same panther walk just in front of my tent. I rose as quietly as I could and, peeping outside, saw it entering Trevelyan's tent. I had my rifle in my hand; I opened the breech quickly to make quite sure the cartridges were there, and then went on tiptoe after the invader. I was terribly afraid it might be a man-eater and would kill Trevelyan before I got there.

"When I reached his *kanat* I pushed it gently on one side and saw the panther standing by Trevelyan's bed. He was sitting up with a look of terror on his face. It seemed to me as if the next moment the panther would spring on my friend and carry him away. I raised my rifle carefully and noiselessly and, aiming at the panther's heart, fired. It sank in a heap on the ground. I rushed in and said: 'Thank God, old chap, I was in time.' To my surprise he did not thank me nor indeed did he speak at all. With an agonised expression he pointed with his finger to the dead animal. I looked and saw a change come over the panther. Its fur disappeared; its forelegs lengthened and became arms; its body shortened, its face lost its bestial shape and became human. Lastly, to my horror, the beast that I had shot changed into the naked corpse of my wife. I turned to Trevelyan and said 'In Heaven's name, what is the meaning of this?' He replied, as if half out of his wits, 'I have behaved like an infernal blackguard, Savile. While pretending to be your friend, I have made love to your wife. On Christmas Day I made her promise to come to my tent that night. This she could do, unseen as I hoped, as you had separate quarters.'

"'You damned sweep, Trevelyan!'

"'Yes, that is just what I was—and well, I was suitably punished. Your wife came about 2 o'clock when I was asleep. I woke up to find her standing by my bedside clad only in my old overcoat. As I put out my arms, she kissed me. I took her into my embrace and she offered no resistance; but when she was about to go I noticed that she had brought no clothes. I asked her what she would do and how she had come. She could not have crossed the open space in the moonlight, mother naked. She laughed and said that she needed no clothes. She stood by the bed without a stitch on and then before my eyes changed slowly into a panther. I was too horrified to say a word and I watched her leave my tent and walk back to her own. I went to bed but I could not sleep. I lay wide awake until morning. Indeed since then I have not slept at all and every night she has come. I have seen her enter as a panther, change into a beautiful woman, and again into a panther. I daresay you have noticed how ill I have looked. I have been on the verge of madness; and now, thank God! you have shot the monster and I am free.'

"Before I could reply, the A.G.G., the Superintendent of Police, Howard and two or three other men crowded into Trevelyan's tent, Howard crying joyfully—'Well, did you get old Spots?— Who fired? Then a hush fell on the group when they saw me, gun in hand, and close in front of me the dead body of my wife, with a hideous expanding bullet wound in her side. The A.G.G. said in a grave, quiet voice: 'Please explain what has happened, Savile.' I replied 'Ask Trevelyan, Sir, he will explain.' Sir William turned to Trevelyan, but he only burst into a fit of maniac laughter: 'He thought he was shooting a panther and he has shot his own wife! Ha! Ha! Ha!'

"Sir William again turned to me said 'You *must* explain, Savile!'

"'It is quite true, Sir, what Trevelyan said. I saw the panther enter his tent. I followed it and, seeing it about to spring on him, I shot it, and now it has turned into my wife. I cannot understand it.'

"'You can hardly expect us to believe that tale, Savile,' said the A.G.G., his lips grimly set. 'I must ask Mr. Jowers, the Superintendent of Police, to do his duty.'

"Jowers stepped forward and arrested me. I was sent back under police guard to Mhow and there I was allowed to engage counsel. I briefed Lawrence and told him the whole story; but it was clear from his expression that he did not believe a word I said.

At last he cried in despair—'Look here, Savile, I am your counsel and, as such, bound to believe what you tell me. Frankly, I cannot; and if I, your advocate, cannot, how can you expect a judge and a jury to do so? So I tell you what: let me conduct your case in my own way. You had plenty of grave and sudden provocation. You were armed as you were sitting up for the panther; and seeing your wife enter Trevelyan's tent at night, you rushed blindly after her, and in a fit of ungovernable rage shot her dead. In France you would be acquitted; even in India the offence will be adjudged culpable homicide not amounting to murder, and you will get two years at the outside.'

"What could I do? My only witness, Trevelyan, had gone raving mad. If my own counsel scoffed at my story, what chance had I with a jury? I should certainly hang. I agreed to plead guilty to a charge of culpable homicide not amounting to murder. After a few formal witnesses had been examined and I had made a statement such as Lawrence had advised, I was convicted on my own plea and sentenced to three years' imprisonment—Lawrence had been unduly optimistic. I got a month or two remission for good conduct and after two and three quarter years in Yeroda jail near Poona, here I am. I have no job and no money."

Savile stopped and rose to his feet as if to stretch himself, and Briggs began to wonder whether it would be possible to squeeze him in as a temporary subordinate in the Forest Department so as to give him a chance to make a fresh start. As he wondered, he saw, or seemed to see, a curious change come over Savile; his yellow coat appeared to be developing round black spots; his fingers that were slender and shapely seemed to be growing into long curved claws; his ears were slipping back to the top of his head and becoming small and pointed; his whole face was jutting out and becoming bestial. Suddenly Savile said with a harsh snarl quite different from the clear cultured voice, in which he had told his story: "And so you will give me all your money, or by God...."

Briggs' brain worked like lightning. He realised that, strong as he was, he would have no chance against the feline monster into which Savile was rapidly turning. Then he remembered that the only animal that a panther fears is a wild buffalo. He pretended to look at something over Savile's shoulder and cried—"Look, look! Buffalo! Buffalo!" Savile swung quickly and nervously round to see. At that moment Briggs sprang to his feet, and with all his strength hit at Savile's jaw. As Briggs rose Savile turned round his head, just in time to receive a tremendous blow on the point of his chin. He collapsed and fell. Briggs, leaving his tiffin basket and its contents where they lay, sprang into his car and pressed the self-starter. Plugs refused to fire, with the result that the car rolled on with only four out of six cylinders working. After a minute or two Briggs looked round anxiously and to his horror saw that the monster—now definitely a panther—had recovered from the blow and was racing after him. He tried to make his car move quicker, but no matter how much he pressed the accelerator, the panther gained on him. At last he felt a shock at the back of the car, and looking round saw the head and forequarters of the panther struggling to climb over the folded hood. He snatched at the cranking handle that lay on the seat at his side and with all his might struck at his enemy's head. The blow caused it to let go the back of the car and it fell to the ground, evidently hurt. Briggs drove on a few hundred yards to where the road rose steeply. He had to drop into second speed and then he looked back again. Once more the panther was following him as hard as it could. In his nervous anxiety to get on, Briggs went back too soon into third speed, with the result that the engine stopped altogether.

"Good God!" muttered Briggs, as the sweat rose on his forehead. "If the self-starter does not work I am lost. I shall never have time to crank up the engine with the handle."

He pressed the self-starter. It gave its usual roar, but no sound came from under the bonnet. Briggs' heart sank into his boots. He pressed again, and this time his heart rejoiced in the answering purr of the working engine. The car again moved forward and in a few seconds reached the top of the slope. Briggs changed into second and then third and, gliding down the hill at full speed, he soon left the panther behind. He looked round and saw his pursuer, just where the road swung outward in a great curve, leap inward to the jungle. He realised then that he was by no means out of danger; for, by taking a short cut through the jungle, the monster would follow the chord while he followed the arc of the semi-circle. An ordinary panther would not have thought of doing so; but it would certainly occur to Savile's diabolic intelligence.

Briggs drove his car as hard as he could; nevertheless, when he reached the point where he expected his enemy to emerge, he unconsciously slowed down to hear, if he could, the soft padding, the only sound a galloping panther makes no matter how thickly the jungle may be strewn with dry leaves. Suddenly he caught the sound quite close to him. In a paroxysm of fear he stamped on the accelerator. This time the old car reacted splendidly. With all its six cylinders working it bounded forward at sixty miles an hour; it was only just in time. suddenly a great yellow body sprang from the forest edge with outstretched paws, missing the back of the car by only a few inches. The road now ran quite straight; the forest began to thin as Briggs neared the outer fringe of the wood. All of a sudden he heard behind him the same well-bred tones in which Savile had entertained him at breakfast.

"Well, goodbye, old chap, and thanks awfully for the lift and the breakfast."

Briggs looked round and there, some three hundred yards away, he saw Savile, just as before, in his yellow well-cut, well-worn shikar suit. Savile spoke again, but this time with a note of irony in his cultured voice which the high trees on each side of the road transmitted like a speaking tube:

"And if you hear of a nice, cushy job, you'll be sure and let me know, won't you? The Dharwar forest will always find me."

With these words and a wave of his hand Savile strolled out of sight into a clearing close by. Briggs drove the rest of the journey in a state very near insanity. He kept repeating to himself interminably the problem suggested by Savile: "Are panther people men who turn themselves into panthers; or are they panthers who turn themselves into men?"

After another hour and a half of furious driving he reached Dharwar. There he drove to the house of his host, the Forest

Superintendent of Dharwar, and when the latter came out to welcome him Briggs asked him excitedly: "I say, Buchan, for God's sake tell me are panther people men who turn themselves into panthers, or panthers who turn themselves into men?"

Buchan, who was a shrewd, kindly Scotsman, did not exclaim as many might have done: "My dear Briggs, what on earth are you talking about?" He saw that Briggs had gone through some very severe experience; so although he had never heard of panther people, he said, like a mother soothing a fretful, questioning child:

"I expect they are men who turn themselves into panthers; after all, a panther would be too stupid to turn itself into a man, wouldn't it?"

There was just enough appearance of logic in this inadequate answer to satisfy Briggs for a moment. Buchan pressed his advantage by adding: "I expect you are very tired. Here, take this whisky and soda and run off for a bath. It's all ready for you; and then we'll have tea and you will tell me the whole story."

Briggs had his whisky and soda and the alcohol and the soothing tones of his host helped to restore his sanity. After he had tubbed and changed, he returned, and during tea he told Buchan his amazing adventure. He then repeated his question as to the origin of panther people.

"Well," said Buchan, "I agree with Savile that it does not really matter, although, judging by his wife's case, it would seem to be the exclusive privilege of humans to turn themselves into panthers. An Indian would say that Mrs. Savile's spirit entered her husband's body after he had shot her; but that only raises the further question whence Mrs. Savile acquired her science. On the other hand, Savile may have invented the story so as to keep you in the forest while he worked up power to change himself into a wild beast. Like your self-starter he may have found it hard to start his internal engine. I tell you what. When you are returning to Dharwar I'll go with you and I'll take with me my six-shooter—none of your popgun pea-shooter Browning automatics—but a real man-stopping Colt six-barrelled revolver and I'll have a cartridge in every barrel. If your friend Savile turns up he'll get something that will check his deplorable versatilities."

Buchan chuckled and Briggs laughed.

As a matter of fact Buchan got no chance of displaying the man-stopping powers of his heavy Colt, for neither of them ever set eyes on Savile. Enquiries at Yeroda jail showed that no Englishman of that name had been imprisoned there. Of course the name 'Savile' may have been assumed; or perhaps Buchan was wrong and Briggs' undesirable acquaintance was really a panther which had somehow or other discovered the art of turning itself into a man, and not a man who knew how to turn himself into a panther.

From *Indian Christmas Stories* (1936)

The Old Graveyard at Sirur

by C.A. Kincaid

WHEN I WAS JUDGE OF POONA SEVERAL YEARS BEFORE the Great War, my tours of inspection used at times to take me to Sirur, the old cantonment some forty miles from Poona that had housed the Poona Horse ever since the conquest of 1818. Not far from the officers' mess and their mud bungalows was the old cemetery. It was no longer used, but it contained the graves of officers of former generations who had succumbed to cholera, enteric fever and the score of other diseases that in eastern lands lie in wait for the English soldier. In the centre rose a tombstone considerably bigger than the others and I often noticed the Indian troopers salute it as they passed. I was loth to question the officers of the Poona Horse, although I knew one or two of them fairly well. It was none of my business and I thought that they might think me impertinent if I probed the matter. One day, however, after seeing several men salute very rigidly with eyes turned towards the central monument, I could no longer control my curiosity; and, meeting a Captain Johnson, an excellent and understanding gentleman, I blurted out:

"Excuse my stupid curiosity; but would you mind telling me why your troopers salute so regularly and so correctly the graveyard. Although they very rightly honour their living superiors, I find it strange that they should salute the dead as well."

"Oh they don't salute the graveyard; they salute old Colonel Hutchings. He commanded the regiment in the eighteen-twenties. He comes out, so they say, and sits on his tomb. It is that big one in the centre. He sits on it and every now and then his wife joins him."

"My dear chap, what are you talking about? They are both dead as doornails. Do you mean their ghosts sit on the tombstone? Have you seen them yourself?"

"Well, I don't know," said Johnson, looking rather confused. "I thought I did once or twice; but it was no doubt my imagination."

"I say, do tell me: who was this Colonel Hutchings? Why does he sit on his tomb? Who was his wife? Why does she sit on his tomb, too?"

"Look here," said Johnson good-humouredly. "I know what an infernal prober you are; but I have neither the time nor the knowledge to stand your cross-examination. You are going into Poona shortly; send for old Rissaldar Major Shinde. I'll write you down his address. He knows all about Colonel Hutchings; he tells us the story after mess sometimes when we ask him to Sirur, as we do once a year at the time of our annual regimental sports. He retired ages ago, but his memory is as fresh as ever."

As Johnson spoke he wrote down the name of the Rissaldar Major and his address in Shukurwar Peth, a well-known quarter in Poona city.

Shortly after my return to headquarters, I sent a line from the Sangam, the judge's official residence, to Rissaldar Major Shinde. I begged him kindly to call on me at 9 a.m. any day that he might be free. I mentioned Captain Johnson's name and told him frankly that I wanted to hear all he could tell me about the cemetery at Sirur, and especially Colonel Hutchings' tomb. Two mornings later a fine old Maratha gentleman drove up in a tonga and was shewn in with every sign of respect by the judge's macebearer.

After shaking my visitor cordially by the hand, I thanked him for coming, and said: "Your name is Shinde, is it not? Are you a member of the family of H.H. the Maharaja of that name?"

"I, Sahib, am a Shinde of Kizarnagar; and you, who have studied our history will remember how the great Madhavrao Shinde would have given up all his titles to be one of my family; but that is another matter. I read in your letter that you wanted to hear about Colonel Hutchings Sahib. He was in a sense more nearly related to me than H.H. the Maharaja; for he married a lady of our family."

"Married a lady of your family? What do you mean, Rissaldar Sahib? He was an Englishman and he could not have married a lady of your family. Nor would her parents have allowed her to marry a Christian no matter who he was."

"Yes, indeed, Sahib, he did, and that was the cause of the trouble. If you care to listen, I shall tell you the story."

"Oh, please do."

"Colonel Hutchings Sahib, so my father used to tell me, was stationed at Kirkee before the Peshwa fought the English in 1818. Hutchings was then a handsome young Captain Sahib and was, it appears, very attractive to our women. One day he and a squadron of horse, mostly recruited from Musulmans and Mhars and all ready to die for their English leader, were riding along the banks of the Muta Mula below where the great dam and bridge now are. It so happened that one of the Shindes of Kizarnagar had died, and, as was then the custom of our family, his widow had given out that she would become a *suttee* and burn with her lord. She was, however, quite a young girl, probably not more than fifteen years of age. When she saw the pyre ready for her to ascend, she lost all control of herself and began to scream and struggle like a maniac. Her mother and married sister tried to soothe her and offered her opium, so that she might be drugged and not feel the pain of burning. But no, Sahib, the widow woman would not listen. One of her brothers wished to stun her with a blow from one of the logs from the pyre; but her mother was reluctant to have this done; for the women of her family—she was a Ghatle from Kolhapur—had never before flinched from the flames. She thought that it would be a disgrace if her daughter did not sit erect on the pyre with her husband's head on her lap and a candle held upright in each hand.

"Just then Hutchings Sahib rode up. The widow, seeing a foreigner, called to him for help. Hutchings Sahib was then a brave young soldier. He did not understand that he was about to insult our holy religion. All he saw was a young and pretty woman, calling to him to save her from a painful death. He turned to his squadron and said: 'Well, brothers, will you help me to carry her out of danger?' Of course those Mlecchas and untouchables were only too pleased. So he charged the crowd. Unarmed, and taken by surprise, they offered little resistance. The dead man's brothers did indeed shew fight; but they were cut down and one of them killed. A couple of Mhars lifted the widow woman in front of Hutchings Sahib's saddle. He turned his horse, rallied his squadron and rode back to Kirkee. There he got a Portuguese padre Sahib, who lived with the Portuguese troops of the Peshwa's army, to marry him to the widow. Thus when the Peshwa's minister complained to Elphinston Sahib, the resident, and demanded the woman back that she might complete the *suttee* ceremony, Elphinston Sahib said that as she had by her second marriage become an Englishwoman and a subject of the king of England, he would not give her up.

"The Peshwa's government told our people and added that owing to the widow woman's remarriage they could do nothing for us. We were furious. The *suttee* ceremony had been stopped. All the merit that would thereby have been acquired by our dead relative had been lost. The widow had been carried off, our kinsmen had been killed, and we were to get no redress. Well, we resolved that if the Peshwa would not help us we should help ourselves.

We vowed that we should kill Hutchings Sahib and the widow woman also."

"You say 'we', Rissaldar Sahib, but you could not have been alive then."

"Quite true, Sahib. I was not born until many years afterwards. I am only seventy years old now. By 'we' I mean the Shindes of Kizarnagar."

"I understand; but do go on, Rissaldar Sahib, with your story."

"As the Sahib pleases. We vowed, as I have said, to kill Hutchings Sahib. It was not, however, easy. Hutchings Sahib and the widow woman lived in a house almost surrounded by the troopers' lines; and as a rumour had spread that we sought their lives, the lines were well guarded and no one allowed inside. One day, it is true, two of our people got through the gates, but before they could do anything they were caught, beaten half dead and thrown out. This added fuel to our hatred; still we could do nothing, for not long afterwards the Peshwa fought the English and they beat him at Kirkee and Ashta. In the end he surrendered and the English, as the Sahib knows, took his country. The Poona Horse were stationed at Sirur. Hutchings Sahib had fought very bravely in the war and he was promoted to command the regiment and to be a Colonel Sahib. He, of course, went to live there too and the widow woman went with him; and all the time we were eating our hearts out with ungratified hatred. It must have been six years after he had risen to command the regiment and was about to return to England that our chance came. We had long hung about Sirur in vain, for he was very cautious. One day, however, when

he went a little way out of Sirur in a *palki,* either to shoot blackbuck
or chinkara, four of our men rushed out of their hiding place in
the dry bed of a river. Slashing the *palki* bearers' legs with our
swords, we made them drop the *palki* and then we fell on the
Colonel and killed him. His gun was unloaded, but he made a great
fight and with his sword wounded two of our men before we could
finish him. This was our undoing; for the *palki* men ran back and
told the widow woman. She told the police that the murderers
must have been Shindes from our village. The police went there
and, finding two of our men with unhealed wounds, arrested them.
They were identified by the *palki* bearers and hanged. We were
now resolved to kill the widow at all costs; but a day or two after
the execution she took opium, died and was buried besides the
Colonel Sahib. The officers raised the big monument that you have
seen over both of them; but they have carved on it only the name
of Hutchings Sahib; for they were ashamed of his marriage to a
woman not of his race. Ever since the Colonel Sahib sits from time
to time on his tomb. Sometimes, although more rarely, the widow
woman sits beside him; so the troopers always salute as they pass
the tomb. Everyone of them has at one time or another seen him
in the spirit."

"So that is the tale, Rissaldar Sahib, thank you ever so much
for it."

"There is no need for thanks, Sahib. It is I who should thank
you for your courteous hearing. Moreover, that is not all the story,
there is more to tell; only no doubt the Sahib is weary and I shall
come again some other day."

"Oh no, Rissaldar Sahib," I said quickly, afraid that I should lose the rest of the yarn. "Do go on. So far from tiring me, your words have made me feel young again."

"The Presence is too kind. Well then I shall continue. Many, many years afterwards we Shindes heard that the son of Colonel Hutchings Sahib's sister, a young man called Furley Sahib, had been posted to the Poona Horse. I was then a youth of twenty years and it was arranged that I should enlist as a trooper in the same regiment and, when the chance came, kill Furley Sahib. I must admit that I was not very eager to do this. The quarrel was all so old and I realized that if my plan succeeded, I should probably be hanged; and that if I failed I should have had to work and train as a soldier for nothing. I did not want to be a soldier. I wanted to stay in Kizarnagar and farm our lands. Still my father and my elder kinsmen put such pressure on me and said so many times that it would be a family disgrace if I did not avenge the honour of the Shindes, that at length I gave way. I joined the Poona Horse as a trooper and after some time I contrived to get myself appointed as an orderly to Furley Sahib. He was a fine young man and I had no feeling of dislike towards him; but I could not escape from the task laid upon me. While I was pondering how to kill him—either by arsenic in his tea or by an open attack on him—war broke out with Afghanistan. Furley Sahib immediately got himself transferred to the 2nd Bombay Cavalry and I asked him to take me with him. I was sure that in a battle I could shoot him without anyone noticing me. Furley Sahib was pleased at my request and we went together by train until we caught up the 2nd Bombay Cavalry near the frontier. I shall not weary the Sahib with a long account of what happened. The Sahib knows the history of the war better than I do. It is enough to say that the 2nd Bombay Cavalry were sent with a body of Indian infantry and the 66th English regiment under General Burrows Sahib to hold Kandahar. Stuart Sahib occupied Kabul. One day Burrows Sahib's scouts told him that Ayub Khan and some five thousand Afghans were assembled in the hills only six or seven miles away. Burrows Sahib decided to attack Ayub Khan and disperse his force before it grew to a great army; for the Afghans were streaming to join Ayub Khan from all quarters. Next morning Burrows Sahib and his brigade moved out against Ayub Khan; but we soon learnt that the scouts had either lied deliberately or had themselves been misled. We went more than twelve miles before we saw the Afghans and then we found that they numbered fifty thousand and not five thousand. Nevertheless Burrows Sahib gave orders to attack; indeed he could hardly have done otherwise, for the enemy were advancing against him at great speed. We of the 2nd Bombay Cavalry were on the right flank and three of the squadrons were commanded by three Monteith brothers, who that day shewed themselves to be real soldiers, very brave and skilful. Suddenly we heard a buzzing noise far away to the left. This was the first rush of the Afghan Ghazis and their shouts reached us in the distance like the hum of bees swarming at the end of the Deccan cold weather. Burrows Sahib formed his infantry into squares and they shot so steadily that the Ghazis were stopped and forced to take cover. Then some minutes later the Ghazis rallied and again charged with the same humming sound.

Again Burrows Sahib formed his men into squares and broke the Ghazi rush with musketry fire. Then that accursed Ayub Khan brought up his guns from behind the hills and before our footsoldiers could deploy into open order, he fired with fury at our squares. Under cover of this fire the Ghazis again charged and our men, confused by the cannonade and with great gaps in their ranks, were not able to stop them as they had done before. Burrows Sahib ordered a retirement; but under the heavy cannon fire and the attacks of the Afghans our infantry broke and it seemed as if our entire army would be destroyed. It was then that the three Monteith brothers shewed such courage and skill. Every time the Ghazis tried to get round the infantry, we of the 2nd Bombay Cavalry charged, each squadron led by a Monteith Sahib. Thus the infantry were able to get back safe to Kandahar. It was during the cavalry fighting that I thought that my chance had come. Lifting my carbine, I took a steady aim at Furley Sahib's back. No one noticed me, as all the troopers were watching the Ghazis and our infantry; I was just about to pull the trigger when I was knocked off my horse by a most violent blow. Some vile Afghan had fired a jezail in our direction and the shot hit me in the chest, just as I was about to shoot Furley Sahib. At first he did not notice my fall, but when the retreat began he saw me on the ground and, lifting me up, put me on the saddle in front of him and so brought me alive to Kandahar. There he looked after me and I soon recovered. By doing this, Furley Sahib wiped out our quarrel, and from that time on I became his devoted friend; and no words of my kinsmen had any influence with me."

"I suppose you were in Kandahar when Lord Roberts marched from Kabul to relieve you."

The old Rissaldar Major drew himself up and saluted on hearing the famous soldier's name: "Yes, indeed I was; the great Roberts Sahib came all the way from Kabul with the speed of Hanuman himself. In the meantime, however, Ayub Khan had tried to take Kandahar by storm and had been beaten back with heavy loss. Many of the Afghans had deserted and we had killed and wounded some ten thousand; so that Lord Roberts Sahib's task was easier than that of Burrows Sahib. Still he did his work thoroughly and so routed that demon of an Ayub Khan that he never fought the English again. That is my whole story."

"Well, thank you ever so much for it; but what happened to Furley Sahib?"

"He got safely through the Afghan War; afterwards he returned to the Poona Horse and rose to command it. It was he who gave me my last promotion and made me a Rissaldar Major. He was like a father to me and after his retirement he wrote to me every Christmas. I felt it deeply when he died, two years ago."

The old man suddenly stopped speaking and his eyes shone with a suspicious moisture.

"Do you think I could photograph Colonel Hutchings on his tomb?" I asked.

The old Rissaldar thought for a moment and said "Yes, I think it is possible. The best time would be at midnight. Two days hence the moon will be full; if the Sahib were to go to the cemetery then, he might catch the Colonel Sahib."

"Splendid! You must come too. I shall drive you there."

"Very well, I shall be happy to do anything that will give the Sahib pleasure."

At nine p.m. two days later the old Rissaldar presented himself at my bungalow ready for the drive to Sirur. As I was about to take the wheel, I noticed that he had no overcoat. It was March and the nights were still chilly and my car was an open one.

" You cannot drive without an overcoat, Rissaldar Sahib; you must take one of mine, otherwise you will catch your death of cold." So saying I ordered my servant to fetch a discarded ulster. I wrapped it round the old warrior and gave him a spare muffler as well to keep his throat warm. He accepted them gratefully. Motorcars did not then move as fast as they do now and it was just on midnight when we reached the Sirur cemetery. We got out and looked at the graveyard from a distance. Seen by the full March moon, it was an awe-inspiring sight.

"Let me go alone, Sahib," whispered the Rissaldar. "Hutchings Sahib may not wish to shew himself to a stranger."

I agreed and the Rissaldar entered the graveyard, while I, concealed among the shrubbery, waited outside. Acting on my instructions, he placed the Kodak on a tomb some thirty feet from the Colonel's monument, gave the film a long exposure and, dropping the shutter, rejoined me. We drove back to Poona and in the small hours parted excellent friends, the Rissaldar returning me my ulster and muffler. I told him to come back in a week's time so that we might examine together the developed proof. Seven days later the peon about nine a.m. announced the Rissaldar. A packet of proofs had arrived the day before, but I had not opened it. I wished to do so in the old man's presence. Among the proofs was that of the Sirur cemetery. I handed it to the Rissaldar without looking at it closely. He cast his eyes over it and exclaimed: "There he is, the Colonel Sahib, there he is! and the widow woman is there, too. I saw them both in the cemetery."

I took the proof from my friend's hands and, sure enough, there, seated on the plinth of the monument, was the shadowy form of an Englishman in old-fashioned dress.

"I see the Colonel Sahib; but where is his wife whom you will call the widow woman?"

"I call her the widow woman," said the Rissaldar Major severely, "because in our caste there is no widow remarriage and she had no right to marry again. Still I see her; she is there coming from behind another tombstone to join him."

I looked where the old soldier pointed and there did seem to be something that might have been the late Mrs. Hutchings. About the Colonel himself there could be no doubt whatever; and I still treasure the photograph of the graveyard, doubly strange because of its weird appearance by moonlight and the uncanny figure of the Englishman sitting on the plinth of the central monument.

I took out my note case and tried to induce the Rissaldar to accept a hundred rupees; but I was severely snubbed. He said with dignity: "A Shinde of Kizarnagar does not accept money for doing an act of courtesy that any gentleman might do for another."

From *Indian Christmas Stories* (1936)

The Munjia

by C.A. Kincaid

IT WAS A STUFFY SEPTEMBER AFTERNOON IN NASIK. RAIN HAD not fallen for some days and even before that it had been far below the average. Indeed, there had at one time been so great a dread of a famine that the priests of Ramachandra's temple had for twenty-four consecutive hours kept their most important idol from resting by pouring cold water over it at short intervals. The suggestion had been made by the English judge, who was immensely respected as a learned Sanskrit scholar. He had supported his suggestion by so many quotations from the Vedas and Puranas (the Hindu gospels and epistles), that the priests had, although with diffidence, followed the Englishman's advice. Its value had been fully vindicated; for within the twentyfour hours a heavy thunderstorm had burst. A week's steady downpour had followed and the earth, soaked with six inches of precious rain, had lost its iron crust and although still thirsting had become soft enough for the early monsoon sowing.

Thus for the present there was no immediate danger of a famine, but sporadic cases of plague had occurred and one of the unlucky sufferers was a young Brahman boy of great promise called Mahadev Joshi. He was a Deshastha Brahman and his school career had been brilliant. He had carried off all the prizes that the Nasik High School could offer. From school he had entered the Deccan College near Poona and there had taken a brilliant first class in mathematics. He had distinguished himself at games as well, and Dr. Selby, the principal of the Deccan College, who loved Mahadev as his own son, had offered him the post of junior professor in mathematics; but the young Brahman was attracted to the Bar, for which his penetrating intellect and perfect knowledge of English were admirably adapted. He presented himself for the High Court pleader's examination and passed it with exceptional brilliancy. Weary of study and anxious to see his parents and friends he had returned to Nasik, the beautiful town near the source of the Godavari river. There, after three weeks of delightful, restful idleness, he had contracted plague. There was nothing strange that he should have done so, for his family house was an old *wada* or mansion dating from the time of the Peshwas and was overrun with rats. The rats were infested with fleas, the fleas settled on the bare feet of the members of the family and thus spread infection; first a servant, next a distant cousin, caught plague. They did not die of it, but they helped to spread the disease; so that when young Mahadev came to the old family house for a holiday, run down from overwork and too little sleep, he was a likely victim.

Mahadev's father Balwantrao and his mother Saraswatibai nursed their sick son with anxious devotion. The father was weighed down by the natural fears that any father would feel for the life of his brilliant son. In the mother's anxiety was a more sinister element. Mahadev had been invested with the sacred thread at the age of twelve and thus had been initiated to the Brahman caste. By the rules of orthodox Hinduism—and Nasik is very orthodox—Mahadev should have been married at fifteen. This is what his mother most ardently wished; indeed the question of his marriage had been fully discussed and he was betrothed to Narmadabai, the pretty daughter of the leading criminal pleader of Ahmadnagar, but old Balwantrao Joshi, greedily ambitious for his son's school and college successes, put off the marriage on various pretexts. His wish was to keep the boy unmarried until his examinations were over. These had now been successfully passed and Balwantrao had drafted wedding invitations that a Bombay printing press would print on cards in big gold letters.

Nevertheless the marriage ceremonies had not begun when Mahadev fell ill, and Saraswatibai was tortured with the thought that if her son died unmarried he would die a "munjia" — a Brahman boy invested with the sacred thread but still a bachelor. She held the vulgar belief that in that event Mahadev's soul would become a vile, evil spirit. Deprived of rebirth because of his parents' sin in delaying his marriage, her darling son would haunt a *pipal* tree and, feared and cursed by every human being, would rush at intervals from his dwelling place and play a horrible trick on some unfortunate person walking close to his tree. His only chance of escape was to possess some wayfarer's body: but she knew how difficult that was. She, therefore prayed and prayed to Vishnu and Ganpati, to Shiva and Parvati and to every other god she could think of—even the graceless Saturn—that her son might recover at any rate live long enough to marry Narmadabai.

The sick boy was well looked after as well as any English patient would have been. The civil surgeon was called in consultation and under his supervision the local practitioner wrote out correct prescriptions. Unhappily there are no specific remedies for plague. What is needed is a perfectly sound constitution, helped by good nursing. Mahadev's mother and sisters were present at his bedside night and day; so he did not lack good nursing. Thanks to their "ceaseless vigilance, the buboes under his armpits grew smaller, and smaller and the sick boy smiled and even laughed, his gaiety spreading joy through the whole household. Then one day he sat up for his morning tea, his mother's arm round his neck; he was bending his head forward to sip it when suddenly he fell forward, knocking the cup and saucer out of her hand. She turned to the towel stand close by for a towel to dry her son's hands and chest; as she did so, Mahadev's body twisted round and fell, so that he hung half in bed and half out of bed. In wild despair Saraswati called to her husband.

"Come, come" she screamed. "Mahadev has fallen, he is very ill!"

Old Balwantrao was deeply immersed in an article in the *Kesari* newspaper condemning vigorously some measure or other proposed by the Government of India. Nevertheless he dropped his paper and ran up the uncarpeted wooden stairs which led to the sleeping rooms. There he saw Mahadev hanging motionless out of bed and Saraswati lying prostrate on his body. He murmured in Marathi "Kay zalen? Kay zalen?" (What has happened? What has happened?) Going to the bedside he lifted his son back into bed and felt his wrist. Afterwards he put his hand on Mahadev's heart. Both pulse and heart were still. With the calm self mastery of the Deccan Brahman, Balwantrao said in even tones: "As it seems to me, Mahadev is dead." Saraswati, half mad with grief, screamed at her husband: "Yes, he is dead and thanks to your wicked ideas, he is dead unmarried, a 'munjia', and he will live on as an evil spirit long after we have died and have been reborn."

"Nonsense! Nonsense! Why believe in such childish tales, 'munjias' do not become evil spirits—that is a mere fable. In any case," he added by way of compromise, "if Mahadev does become a demon we can always appease him by offering him rice and grain, or even a fowl now and then."

No words of Balwantrao, however soothing, could lessen the poor mother's grief. Had her darling son died married she would probably have borne her sorrow and survived; but the dreadful thought that her beloved son should, from being an universal favourite in school, college and in Nasik society, become a hateful phantom, proved too much for Saraswati. When Balwantrao and the male mourners returned from the burning ground whither they had taken Mahadev's body, they found his mother lying face downwards at the bottom of the stairs. A cerebral hemorrhage had overtaken her as she was walking up to take a last look at her son's room. She had fallen backwards and broken her neck in her fall. A day later her body was carried to the same burning ground wherein Mahadev's had already been consumed.

Poor old Balwantrao shaved his head and moustaches and observed the usual twelve days' mourning. He sought refuge from his grief in the devotion of his daughters and in the study of sacred Sanskrit books; and he gave little thought to the question that the other townspeople were feverishly asking each other; "Where will the 'munjia' take up his abode?"

For many days after the death of Mahadev the Nasik townsmen put red painted stones at the foot of various *pipal* trees in the neighbourhood of the town. One or two trees near Nasik were, it was believed, already occupied by 'munjias' and they received due homage and small daily offerings of rice. It never occurred to any of the citizens that the new 'munjia' would go any distance from the city. They did not bear in mind that Mahadev, who had often mixed with Englishmen and liked them, might well establish himself near the quarter where they lived. One evening two or three tongas, filled with respectable Brahmans of Nasik and their wives and families, set out about 10 p.m. to catch the midnight express from Nasik Road Station. The train reached Bombay at 8 a.m. next morning and night travel saved the passengers, all of whom slept well in trains, the hot day journey down the Ghats and through the Konkan plain. The third class carriages can be very stuffy by day and Indian children suffer a good deal from the heat.

The road to the station ran west of the Nasik golf course, used alike by Bombay visitors and Nasik residents. Between the road and the links stood a giant *pipal* tree. It was full moon and the travellers were laughing and talking together, holding in their hands endless bundles of bedding and balancing their sterns precariously on innumerable tin trunks and brass waterpots. As the tongas passed the *pipal* tree the ponies took fright and galloping madly off the road and across the open country, they did not stop until they had overturned the tongas into a ravine a mile away. No fewer than two children and a young woman were killed outright. One man had a compound fracture of the leg, a second had his arm broken and everyone, including the drivers, was badly shaken and injured. The ponies were put on their feet, shivering with fright, but beyond a few slight cuts were not badly injured. The police were sent for; the dead were transported to the mortuary near the Civil Hospital. The injured were handed over to the care of the house surgeon and next day the police inspector held an inquest. There was, however, little to record save the bare facts of the accident. The oldest Brahman assured the inspector that he had heard a bloodcurdling shriek and that in the moonlight he had seen a monstrous diabolical figure issue from the *pipal* tree and deliberately scare the ponies. In his judgment the phantom was the soul of Mahadev, the 'munjia' that had taken up an abode in the *pipal* tree on the golf course.

The Brahman was corroborated by one or two of the women and one of the older men; nevertheless the inspector refused to put into his report anything about the 'munjia'. He had experienced the unpleasant scepticism of English officials and he knew well that any reference to such a phenomenon would only be treated by his English superior as "damned native superstition" and that he himself would get a "wigging" for writing rubbish in an inquest report.

The refusal of the inspector to record the evidence of the elderly Brahman was fully understood by the Nasik townsmen and they were not annoyed by it. After all, what could the superintendent do, even if he knew that a 'munjia' haunted the *pipal* tree? He might have the tree cut down, but that would only infuriate the demon who lived in it. Mahadev's soul would seek some other hiding place and issuing therefrom would cause worse trouble than ever. No; the townsmen's course was clear. They knew now where the 'munjia' dwelt and it was for them to propitiate him by worshipping him as a god, by placing beneath his tree stones painted with the royal red of divinity, by offering him daily small portions of rice and by burning nightly in his honour small single-wick lamps full of country oil.

Such attention might well have soothed the irascible spirit of any ordinary 'munjia'; but Mahadev, whose acute intelligence had survived his body, knew well that such offerings, although pleasing, got a 'munjia' nowhere. His only chance of obtaining a speedy rebirth and thus advancing towards the end of his eighty million earthly lives was to enter and possess some other human body and then cause its destruction. There were several ways of possessing a human body, but only one was easy and that was to enter the mouth when its owner yawned. Mahadev, no longer anxious to do anyone harm now that offerings were made at the foot of the *pipal* tree, hovered about the neighbourhood, hoping to take advantage of some passing Indian and to possess his body when he yawned. Unfortunately every Indian is well aware of the risks run in yawning and always snaps his fingers in front of his mouth so as to scare away evil spirits.

For a whole month Mahadev's spirit fluttered close to the faces of passing wayfarers, but not one gave him a chance. They did not often yawn; but when they did they never failed to snap their fingers and to scare him away. At last seeing a solitary Englishman yawn cavernously in the distance it occurred to Mahadev that he might possess an Englishman's body, since he could not enter an Indian's. At first the thought was hateful to him. Although he had often met Englishmen and liked many of them, he had always remained orthodox in food and the thought of occupying the body of a "beef-eating" foreigner was simply hateful. Nevertheless he decided at last that it was better to enter an Englishman's body and drive out his soul than remain for ever an 'anima sine corpore,' gibbering dismally in a *pipal* tree.

When, however, he lay in wait for Englishmen playing golf, he found another obstacle in his way. When they yawned, especially if they were not alone, they put a hand in front of their mouth, thus blocking the entrance quite as effectually as by snapping their fingers. Still Mahadev had seen one Englishman yawn without covering his mouth, so he hoped that he would see another; and so it happened. After several days' vain waiting, Mahadev saw the Assistant Judge Colin Travers pass close to the *pipal* tree. Travers had come out of court late and had, therefore, found no partner at the clubhouse. He was tired with work and had a yawning fit. As he passed the *pipal* tree he yawned for about the tenth time. He was carrying in one hand a mashie and in the other a bag of clubs, so he had no hand left with which to cover his mouth. It opened to its fullest extent and offered a wide aperture by which Mahadev could enter. The 'munjia' dived between the double row of strong, white teeth, down the throat; and while Colin Travers was laying down his bag of clubs and wondering whether he should play his next shot with his mashie or his iron, the evil spirit that had been Mahadev drove out Colin Travers' soul and occupied the vacant body.

The physical shock to Travers was so great that he sat down helplessly at the foot of the *pipal* tree and gasped feebly for breath. Once, however, he recovered his physical powers he became the tool of Mahadev's spirit and obeyed without hesitation the 'munjia's' slightest whim. Indeed, why should he have objected? His own soul was lost and had no longer any control over his body; on the other hand Mahadev's soul completely dominated it. Now what Mahadev wanted was that his new body should be destroyed. His own spirit would then be free for rebirth. There were two ways by which the 'munjia' could achieve his end. He might either kill himself or he might commit a murder and get hanged. Now in the Hindu belief suicide (athmaghat) is a grave sin and Mahadev had already committed sin enough by entering the soul of an Englishman. In his next life he would certainly have to pay for that crime by not being born a Brahman. If he committed suicide as well, heaven alone knew what dreadful fate might befall him. He might be reborn as a Mhar or even as a Mang. His only resource, therefore, was to commit a murder and so get condemned to death. Having formed this resolve, he picked up his clubs and walking towards the assistant judge's bungalow, entered it. The servants seeing, as they thought, their master Colin Travers, salaamed and made way for him. The 'munjia' did not know Mrs. Travers, but he hoped that he would find her in. She was sitting in the dining room with a friend, a lady missionary from the medical mission beyond Godavari. Hearing her husband's step, she called 'Is that you Colin? I thought you were going to the Club. Miss Smith the medical missionary is here. She will be delighted to see you. Do come and talk to her."

"Oh! do, Mr. Travers" echoed Miss Smith.

The 'munjia' noticed a thrusting dagger on the wall just inside the outer door. Travers had secured it when trying some dacoits. The 'munjia' took it off the wall, felt its point and walked into the drawing room. He bent over Mrs. Travers, as if to kiss her, but she recoiled in horror at the expression of his eyes.

"Good gracious, Colin, what is the matter with you? You look different! You have become somebody else!"

The false Colin did not answer, but deliberately drove his; thrusting dagger into her heart. The unfortunate missionary rose to flee, but the 'munjia' overtook her and killed her with a thrust in the back. He then threw the dagger on the ground, walked to the office of the superintendent of police, Alfred Dawkins and said calmly: "I have come to give myself up for a double murder, please arrest me."

The superintendent had for several hours been trying to pen a report about the criminal tribes in his district. He had a store of sound practical knowledge of their ways and customs and he could have told at a glance to what section any wandering beggar belonged; but his penmanship was not equal to his experience. In his efforts to cover two sheets of foolscap with material that a skilled writer could have expanded into a thick book, the unhappy superintendent had chewed his wooden penholder almost down to the metal. He was too preoccupied to grasp what Travers had said: but delighted to escape for a moment from the intolerable drudgery of writing sonorous official phrases, he rose to his feet and said cordially: "By Jove, Travers, do come in; sit down and have a whisky and soda! Here, boy, bring in two chota pegs. I suppose you have come to speak to me about the police enquiry in that coining case? Or let me see—would it be about the murder of little Krishnabai by that up-country watchman?"

"No indeed, I have not come about either of those cases, Superintendent Sahib," said Travers, using unconsciously the Indian form of address, " I have just committed a double murder and I have come to give myself up."

"Committed a double murder? What the devil are you talking about? If you have come to pull my leg, old chap, I really have no time now and you'd better try your luck some other day; but don't go away until you've had your chota peg. It's no fun drinking alone, is it? Ha! Ha!" and the jolly policeman laughed heartily.

"No, Superintendent Sahib, I am not joking," replied Travers earnestly. "I really have committed a double murder and please come and see for yourself."

After a quarter of an hour Dawkins, clad in white uniform and followed by four constables, joined Travers.

"Now come along and show me this mare's nest of yours."

Travers did not reply and the two walked together in silence during the ten minutes needed to go from the superintendent's house to that of the assistant judge. On reaching it, they were met by a mob of excited servants, who shouted: "The Sahib has killed his Memsahib and the doctor Memsahib! The Sahib has killed his Memsahib and the doctor Memsahib!"

The superintendent began at last to think that there was something in Travers' story and entering the assistant judge's bungalow became certain of its truth.

Turning to one of the constables, Dawkins told him to fetch the deputy superintendent of police, Khan Sahib Mahmud Khan, and instruct him to hold an inquest. With two constables behind them he and Travers walked to the Khan Bahadur's house. The latter, a retired Parsi Deputy Collector, nearly fell over backwards when he was asked to record Travers' confession.

"The fact was," stated Travers, " I was both tired of my wife and jealous of her. I wanted to get rid of her; I also wished to punish her for the way she flirted with....with (the 'munjia' did not know the names of any of the regimental officers, so he finished lamely) with certain military gentlemen. Coming home I saw her sitting in the drawing room, so I decided to kill her. I took a dacoit's dagger from off the wall and going up to her, I stabbed her. Then that foolish woman, Miss Smith began to talk, you know how these medical missionaries jabber—so I killed her too."

The confession was carefully recorded. Travers was placed in the lockup for the night; and next morning he was taken before the first class assistant collector, to whom the superintendent had telegraphed. He recorded the Crown evidence as briefly as possible; and when Travers pleaded guilty to the two charges of murder and admitted the correctness of his confession, the magistrate committed the accused to take his trial in the High Court of Bombay.

On the morning of Travers' trial there was great excitement in the Presidency town. The sessions hall of the High Court of Judicature was packed to overflowing; indeed hundreds of would-be spectators were turned away. Travers' trial was the first on the list of criminal trials. The judge to whom the sessions had been allotted sat in state in his red robes under the sword of justice. On either side sat the Sheriff and the Chief Presidency Magistrate. As Travers was English, the jury of nine selected to find on his guilt or innocence were also English. He had refused to engage a barrister, so one of the European members of the Bar, who knew him personally, undertook voluntarily his defence. It was impossible for his counsel to do much, because Travers from the beginning insisted on pleading guilty; the medical evidence, too, confirmed the accused's protest that he was absolutely sane. The barrister for the defence could only rely on the passage in Travers' confession that he was jealous and attempted to reduce, the charge from one of murder to one of culpable homicide; but as the Advocate-General pointed out, Travers' jealousy of his wife was no excuse for the assassination of Miss Smith. The judge summed up shortly and the jury after an absence of barely ten minutes brought in a verdict that Travers was guilty of murder, but added to their verdict a strong recommendation for mercy. Why they did so, they would probably have found it hard to explain. Their real reason, no doubt, was that in their belief no sane man could have behaved like Travers. If Travers was sane, then all the facts had not been put before the court.

The judge was glad of an excuse not to pass sentence of death on a man whom he knew personally and whom he had until recently always esteemed; so much to Travers' obvious disgust, he passed a sentence of penal servitude for life. The accused was led away and the judge called the next case.

Travers was sent to jail and from the first was an object of special interest to the superintendent, Captain Jameson of the Indian Medical Service. Jameson had never met Travers before, but he felt that there must be some terrible secret underlying his conduct. The prison staff took their cue from the superintendent, Travers responded to kindness and the jail officials all thought he was the nicest as well as the most intelligent prisoner, whom they had ever had at Euroda. It was however, only the lull before the storm. The 'munjia' had not the slightest intention of remaining imprisoned in Travers' body a moment longer than he could help. If two murders did not suffice to procure a death sentence, then he would commit three. The third would certainly bring him release, for murder by a life convict can, under the Indian Penal Code, only be punished by death. One day Travers asked if he might have a pair of Indian clubs for morning exercise, as, so he said, his health was suffering from lack of it. He had always been accustomed to swing them for half an hour every morning. Jameson was delighted to grant this trifling indulgence and as he had a spare pair in his bungalow, he brought them over the same evening and gave them to Travers.

Travers broke into profuse thanks, so as to disarm any possible fears on the superintendent's part. Picking up the clubs, he swung them once over his shoulder and then brought down with all his force the right hand club on the top of Jameson's head. The unfortunate officer fell with a broken skull; and a second blow, as he lay on the hard stone flagged courtyard shattered it to pieces.

"Now," thought the 'munjia' in triumph, "I am bound to be hanged."

No one, however, came forward to arrest him. The guards were all too bewildered to take any action. Then the joy of battle inherited from Travers' Norse ancestors acted physically on Mahadev's soul. "After all why await trial? Why not go on killing until death comes of itself?" With a club in each hand Travers fell on the unfortunate Maratha guard, who scattered in every direction. Running after them at great speed, Travers overtook several and with mighty blows clubbed them to death. The Indian convicts locked into their cells were in an ecstasy of delight. They applauded each murderous blow with yells of:

"Shabash Sahib! Maro Sahib!" (Bravo Sahib! Hit them Sahib)!

After Travers had killed half a dozen sepoys, those on duty at the outer gate ran up the staircase into the central tower, whence they commanded all the open spaces of the great prison. From this vantage point, they took careful aim with their rifles and fired deliberately at Travers. It was not easy to kill him, because he was moving about and also because in his berserk rage, he did not seem to be affected by the bullet wounds. At last he collapsed suddenly from loss of blood. As he lay motionless the guards fired a volley at him. He gave a convulsive movement, tried to rise and fell back dead.

At last the 'munjia' had won the desired release. Mahadev's soul left Travers' body and took its place in the line of Hindu souls waiting for reincarnation.

All the Englishmen who had known Travers were deeply shocked at his crimes and death.

"Such a terrible end to a most promising career," they said. "Travers might have risen to anything. He must have been mad but it was a dreadful end."

Yes, they were quite right; it was a dreadful end, a terrible end. Yet what happened to Travers might have happened to anyone— to you or to me.

From *Indian Christmas Stories (1936)*

The Pool

by John Eyton

SOME THREE HUNDRED YEARS AGO A LITTLE WHITE TEMPLE nestled in a fold of the hills, like a mushroom in a green dell. It stood on the bank of a dark pool; wooded hills towered over it to the west, and barren hills rolled away to the east. It was a very holy place; men believed that the foot of God had touched earth here and had made a valley. So from time immemorial it had been a place of pilgrimage. Men journeyed to the hills to see it, and the steps leading down to the pool were often thronged with travellers in white garments, women in saris of red and blue, sadhus in orange and in yellow.

The water was dark—born of a deep-laid spring, which was never dry, and whose overflow ran away in a little tinkling rill into

the deep woods. It was believed that the pool was bottomless—
for what could resist the foot of God?

Animals came to drink quite near the temple with out fear—
dark, great-eyed Sambar stags—little barking deer of the colour
of autumn leaves—mottled leopards. There were bright birds too
about it—proud pheasants, and jays of vivid blue; big butterflies
of dark green and blue, with swallow tails; and red dragon-flies
haunted the reedy edges.

It was ever a place of great silence and of rest. A very holy man
watched over the temple, sitting all day long, legs crossed, arms
folded. He was said to be a hundred years old. His face was
wizened and shrivelled and puckered in a thousand wrinkles. His
head was shaven, and his forehead bore three upright lines of
yellow paint. He wore but a single blanket of faded orange.

Such were the temple and the pool, and the priest of the pool.

There came an evil day for that peaceful place. A horde of wild
Mohammedan fanatics from below swept over the hills and
descended like a scourge on the pool. The little old priest ran up
the path towards them, his arms outstretched, adjuring them to
spare the ancient holy temple. A swarthy man of great stature lifted
his sharp sword and swept off the head of the little priest; others
plunged their swords into the frail body, and they threw the wreck
of it into the pool. They burned the temple and destroyed the
peace of the place..... Then the pestilence passed on.

Thereafter, green rushes covered the whole face of the water,
save where the spring welled up in the middle. Men feared to
approach the pool, where pale figures were seen at night, and
where a despairing cry was sometimes heard. The peace returned;

the place was left to the animals and the birds and the butterflies. But the memory of it never died.

Time passed, and the surrounding hills came into the hands of an Englishman, a retired Colonel named Brown. He was not an unkindly man, but he had a strong belief in the absolute superiority of his own race, and in the inviolability of property. He was tall, with white hair and moustache, and a face whose natural redness was enhanced by the white suits and hats which he wore. He made a pleasant estate in the hills; built a roomy bungalow; put up neat cottages; planted orchards, laid out paths everywhere; in fact, subdued the jungle with a system admirably English. Incidentally he cleaned up the pool, which lay just beyond his boundary. The villagers refused to do the work, but he imported labour, and cleared out the rushes and dredged up the mud. In the course of the work they found a number of blackened stones and rudely carved figures, which the Colonel gave to the Lucknow Museum. Evidently there had been some sort of a temple on the spot, which lent colour to the village talk. Then the spring was analysed and found to contain good water; so the supply was utilised, pipe-lines being laid on to the gardens. The villagers resented the whole proceeding, but they always did resent innovation. Colonel Brown was justly proud of his improvements.

Then the most annoying thing happened. The Colonel was walking round the estate one afternoon when he distinctly heard the mournful chant which accompanies funeral procession. It was the usual thing—a sentence endlessly repeated by two alternate groups, first in full tone, then faintly, like an echo. It came from the direction of the pool. When he had turned the corner he saw the awful truth—a little party of men walking swiftly down the path and bearing a stretcher on which lay a body swathed in white. Mourners trotted behind intoning their sad chant. They were actually going to burn a dead body near the spring-head! It was monstrous. They did it too; he saw the smoke curling up from the valley, and found logs of charred wood at the fringe of the pool the next morning.

That afternoon was the beginning of the Colonel's troubles. First he put a chowkidar on the place, and the chowkidar was beaten by day and saw bhuts by night and ran away. But the burning went on, in proportion to the mortality of the village. Then the Colonel summoned the head men, who talked nonsense about the place being holy from time immemorial. He dismissed them with a purple face and a few home truths. Next, he applied to the civil authorities, who declined to interfere, since the pool was not actually on the estate of Colonel Brown, and had certainly a reputed sanctity. Lastly, he wrote to the *Pioneer*—last resource of wounded pride—and complained of 'the new spirit of pandering to the native, regardless of the position and rights of landlords,' and wondered what the Government was doing.

In spite of all, the burning continued. People refused to burn anywhere else. They believed that here was sanctity for their dead.

Then worse befell. One morning the Colonel observed through his field-glasses a little strip of red rag floating from a tree on the margin of the pool. This would not appear to be of importance; but the Colonel knew India. That red rag meant a priest, and a priest meant pilgrimage. Never was proud banner a surer challenge than was that little strip of red rag. The red rag affected the Colonel after the proverbial manner. He descended on the place, breathing unutterable things.

All he found was a solitary figure sitting under the tree which flaunted the red rag. It was a man of middle age, clad in a blanket of faded yellow; his head was clean-shaven, and his forehead bore three upright lines of yellow paint. He sat motionless, with set, staring eyes. The Colonel asked him his business... no answer; Then he made a sort of set speech on the rights of man... still no answer; then he began to shout, but the priest still ignored his presence. He failed to make any impression on that holy man. Angry as he felt, he knew better than to lay lands on a priest— so he marched off, speechless with rage. They would build a temple next, he knew, if they were given a chance. So he stalked home and wrote a perfect sheaf of letters and appeals on the subject.

That evening the Colonel began a nasty attack of malaria. It is possible that he had been bitten by a mosquito on the occasion of one of his numerous visits to the pool, which was still a swampy place, hot and stuffy. However this may be, the mosquito which bit the Colonel knew his business. He was in bed a fortnight. His wife barely managed to pull him through the attack which was unusually malignant. When he could get about again, his first walk was in the direction of the pool....

There, like a mushroom in a green dell, nestled a little new white temple.

With the reader's indulgence, the author begs leave to draw a picture dating some three hundred years hence....

Colonel Brown is long forgotten. The Englishman, and his Government, and his rights, and his laws have faded away as a ripple dies on water—as a wind stirs in the trees and is gone. But on the bank of the dark pool a little white temple still stands, and still the pilgrims come... for such is India.